Secrets in New York

a contemporary romantic novella

by Philippa Carey

Secrets in New York, copyright © 2020
by Philippa Carey

Philippa Carey has asserted her right to be identified as the author of this Work in accordance with the Copyright, Designs and Patents Act 1988.

All rights reserved. No part of this publication may be reproduced, distributed, or transmitted in any form or by any means, including photocopying, recording, or other electronic or mechanical methods, without the prior written permission of the copyright holder, except in the case of brief quotations embodied in critical reviews and certain other non commercial uses permitted by copyright law. For permission requests, email the author at the address below.

This book is sold subject to the condition that it shall not, by way of trade or otherwise, be lent, resold, hired out, or otherwise circulated without the author's prior consent in any form of binding or cover other than that in which it is published and without a similar condition being imposed on the subsequent purchaser.

This is a work of fiction. All names, characters, events and places other than those clearly in the public domain, spring entirely from the author's own imagination and any resemblance to actual persons, living or dead, is coincidental.

Second Edition published by Idyllic Books, UK.

All enquiries to enquiries@idyllic-books.uk

Chapter 1

It was Wednesday morning and Vincent Kingsley sat in his pyjamas and dressing gown on the edge of his sister's bed. His elbows were on his knees, his face in his hands and his blond hair was hanging down in front of his face. Just when everything was arranged for their trip tomorrow, fate had thrown a spanner in the works.

"It's going to be a disaster," he moaned, "it was so hard to get the contract in the first place and now you can be sure they won't renew it."

His twin sister Valerie was sitting in the bed, propped up on some pillows. Her matching blond hair was lank with perspiration and she was rather obviously running a high fever. All her muscles ached and she felt too tired to argue.

"It will be fine," she croaked.

She sipped a little water from a glass on the bedside table, before continuing, "you're just being a drama queen and exaggerating. Email them to say I have flu and can't go, but you will be going there in any case."

She paused for a moment to catch her breath before continuing again.

"Lots of people have flu at the moment. Speaking of which, you had better keep your distance, otherwise you'll get it too. Tell them we'll both be there next time."

She knew her brother would not take kindly to being called a drama queen and he promptly sat up and brushed his hair from his face. Valerie knew her twin well and how to needle him into action.

"There may not be a next time," he muttered.

He turned to face Valerie and wagged his finger at her.

"You know what they said, 'If Valerie Kay doesn't appear at the conference this time, do a book signing and promote her third book, they won't be publishing any fourth book'. I hardly think they will see her agent turning up as a suitable substitute, will they? I mean, I can't show up and say 'oh, by the way, I'm the author and my sister is the agent, not the other way around'. We both know Julia Wynne thinks there is no place in romantic fiction for a man. She barely tolerates me as the supposed agent and then only because I'm your twin brother."

He stopped waving his hands in the air in frustration and smacked them down onto his knees.

Valerie felt exhausted already and could argue no more.

"Oh just go and pack your bag," she said wearily, "there's nothing to lose by going, your plane ticket is non-refundable and it shows willing by you turning up, so you might as well go. Now go away and leave me in peace, I need to sleep."

She slid down in the bed and pushed at his hip with a foot.

"Go away and send that email," she mumbled from under the covers.

Vincent stood and headed towards the door grumbling to himself, "I suppose so, but knowing my luck I'll have flu tomorrow as well."

He paused in the doorway and turned back to face Valerie.

"I'll call mum and ask her to come over

tomorrow afternoon and see how you are."

Valerie dismissed him with a limp wave of her hand.

Vincent and Valerie had gone to Cambridge University together and both of them had joined Clare College. Valerie had obtained a good degree in biochemistry and now worked for a major pharmaceutical company in London. Vincent, however, had graduated in English Literature and in his second year had started writing romance novels as a sideline. He had quickly discovered that nobody took him seriously, firstly because 'trashy romance' wasn't 'proper' writing, secondly, because men don't read romantic novels and therefore, thirdly, they can't possibly write romantic fiction can they?

He solved the problem by pretending Valerie was the author, writing as Valerie Kay, and he was merely her agent, Vincent Kingsley. Thus he had his first book accepted for publication before he had even graduated. Now, nearly two years later, his third book had just been released, completing his initial contract with the publisher. His fourth book was mostly written and he was hoping to negotiate better terms in a new contract. Maintaining the charade had been made easier by them sharing a house in Wimbledon, South London, while their publisher was based in Los Angeles.

Philippa Carey

Chapter 2

It was mid-afternoon in California when a head popped up over the wall of Carmen Castro's office cubicle.

"CC, you're to go upstairs to see Julia Wynne straightaway," said the head.

"Do you know why?" asked Carmen, pushing back from her desk and computer.

"Nope, I was just told to tell you on my way past. Bye!"

The head vanished and then popped up again.

"I hope you don't need it, but just in case, good luck!"

The head vanished again.

Carmen sagged in her chair. She thought this could only be bad news. This was her first job and it wasn't going nearly as well as it could. Just this summer she had graduated from Stanford University with a major in English Literature and been pleased to get this job in Los Angeles within easy reach of her family. She had met Julia Wynne, the Vice President of the Romance Division, only once before, on the day she joined the publisher two months ago.

Carmen wondered if maybe the incident with the broken photocopier yesterday had come to Julia's attention. It really wasn't Carmen's fault, it was a bad design feature and bound to break sooner or later.

Or perhaps it was the water cooler bottle she dropped and broke in the stairwell last week. That really wasn't her fault either. The bottles were too heavy and nobody had told her she should get the janitor to carry it.

Then there was the time all the paper cascaded off the shelf in the stockroom. How was she to know there was a stepladder stored behind the door and the shelves weren't fixed to the brackets?

And then... Carmen sighed sadly. It was no good re-living all the embarrassing incidents. She was obviously going to get fired and the boss was going to have to do it, as her manager was off sick with flu, like many other people in the office. There was nothing she could do now she thought, so she might as well get it over with. She stood up and surveyed her desk. Should she put all her personal stuff in a box right now, she wondered? No, she told herself, surely they had to let her collect it on the way out, even if she had an escort to the door. She tucked her hair behind her ears, straightened her blouse, brushed her skirt down then turned and reluctantly headed for the stairwell.

She dragged herself two floors up and arrived outside Julia's office. The door was open and Julia was talking with her secretary, both of them bent over some papers on the desk. Carmen hoped it wouldn't take long and be full of recriminations and reprimands. It was horrible enough as it was. She took a deep breath, stood up straight and tapped on the door. Julia and the secretary glanced up and Julia beckoned her to come in. She pointed at the chair in front of her desk as she finished talking to her secretary.

Carmen crossed what felt like a mile of carpet

and perched on the edge of the chair. The secretary straightened up, picked up some of the sheets of paper and left the office, closing the door behind her. Carmen clutched her hands in her lap and swallowed, as Julia looked up and smiled. Smiled? It wasn't quite what Carmen was expecting, but who knows? She had heard a lot of unflattering comments and maybe Julia enjoyed sacking people?

"Carmen, I need you to go to New York tomorrow and help at the conference, is it a problem?"

"No, no, I can do that," stuttered Carmen in amazement.

If she was keeping her job, there definitely wouldn't be a problem and her diary would get erased as soon as she got back to her cubicle.

"What do you need me to do?"

"It's the flu epidemic. People are dropping like flies everywhere and we're short handed in New York. I know you've only been with us a short while, but you seem to have initiative."

She paused and looked at Carmen meaningfully.

"Sometimes you might have had too much initiative and be reluctant to ask for help, but I'm told you're smart, so I'm hoping you'll get the balance right after a while."

Carmen blushed and opened her mouth to explain things.

Julia held up her hand and Carmen closed her mouth again.

"Never mind history, none of it is very important now. Get yourself to New York, find Elizabeth from the New York office and she'll tell you what to do. In the meantime, take these."

Julia handed Carmen the remaining sheets of paper from her desk.

"Some of the authors we invited can't make it because of the flu epidemic and the rooming lists need changing. Most of them are twin rooms to keep our costs down. Take the list of substitutes, put them where names have been crossed out and call the hotel this afternoon with the changes, so as to be sure it's done before anyone gets to the hotel. When you've done that come back and collect a plane ticket and some cash from Patty my secretary. Any questions?"

Carmen thought quickly as she recovered from her surprise.

"Anybody I should or should not put together? And has anybody called the substitutes and made sure they are going?"

Julia smiled, looking pleased at Carmen's questions.

"Don't worry, Patty will be calling them now and they will no doubt be grateful for the invite and free room. If any of them have flu as well, she'll let you know when you pick up the tickets. You'll have to call the hotel with any last minute changes before you leave today, because New York is three hours ahead of us. One of those pages is a note of who should and shouldn't be together. Make sure you keep that to yourself. Anything else?"

Carmen looked up.

"No, I don't think so," she said thoughtfully. "Oh

wait! What should I wear?"

Julia looked up and down at Carmen.

"What you're wearing now is fine for the day," said Julia, "but take a smart dress for the presentation dinner and some jeans or something for the line dancing evening. If you have any other questions call me or Patty, otherwise drop whatever else you were working on and get started with this."

"Right, thank you," said Carmen, standing and heading for the door.

"And remember," said Julia as Carmen opened the door, "if you need something, don't hesitate to ask, you don't have to do absolutely everything yourself."

Carmen looked back, nodded in embarrassment and quickly left the office, closing the door quietly behind her. She headed for the stairs in a daze. As soon as she was out of sight she skipped and punched the air, mouthing, 'Yes!' Not only was she not fired, but she had been given something important to do!

Back at her desk, Carmen pushed everything else to one side and put the sheets of paper on her desk to study. This didn't look too hard. Seven no-shows and six new names, plus herself. As she made the changes she noticed an earlier mistake: There were two names the same but one was now crossed out, so really it had been six flu victims and one mistake. She looked thoughtfully at the name which had been duplicated. It was V Kingsley and she was fairly sure this was Valerie Kay whose third book she had just finished reading. Carmen was a fan of Valerie Kay.

You wouldn't want a fan sharing an author's room, would you? But Carmen was staff, so it was ok wasn't it? Besides, Valerie was from the United Kingdom and this might be the only chance for Carmen to meet her. Carmen put her own name against the space and made a mental note to take her own copies of Valerie's first three books to get them autographed.

She filled in the remaining names, checked on the other list there were no sensitive conflicts and picked up the phone to change the hotel reservations. Less than an hour later she was back at Patty's desk, feeling a lot more positive than before.

"Everything is fine, there are no more changes," said Patty.

She handed Carmen an open envelope. There's some cash in there, get receipts for what you spend and come see me when you get back to settle the expenses. I've put you on the mid-day flight to JFK in case you still have anything to do in the morning. You'll get to New York late, so make sure the hotel knows you're arriving late, then just take a cab to the hotel from the airport. I suggest you take a carry-on bag only so as to save time. Also don't forget to take photo id like a driver's license for check-in at the airport. Do you need a cab to get to LAX?"

Carmen took the envelope.

"No, there's no need for a cab. I'm only in Santa Monica, I can get the bus."

Patty waved her hand dismissively and smiled at Carmen,

"Oh, don't bother with the bus. The company is paying, just take a cab in the morning. Have a good

trip and I'll see you when you get back."
Carmen returned her smile.
"Thanks, I'll see you on Tuesday!"

Philippa Carey

12

Chapter 3

Vincent got to the hotel in Manhattan by seven in the evening, feeling totally washed out. He hoped it wasn't flu, but just a mixture of jet lag, the stress of travel and worrying about both his twin sister Valerie and the conference. At least he knew Valerie was managing with help from their mother, as he had called them as soon as he had arrived at JFK. He got the card key from hotel reception and dragged himself up to the room. Vincent debated what to do, as the clock said seven, but his body said midnight. In the end he concluded he might as well sleep, as it wasn't worth trying to adjust to local time simply for a long weekend. And if it was flu, sleep might be the way to shake it off. He opened his suitcase, but didn't bother to unpack anything except for taking his toiletries bag out. He then closed the window drapes, stripped, cleaned his teeth and fell into the bed which was nearest the window and the bathroom. No sooner than he had turned out the light but he was sound asleep.

Carmen didn't get to the hotel until midnight after a five hour flight, three hour time difference and the transfer from JFK. She knew she would have to be up early in the morning to start work for the conference, so she didn't waste any time before getting her key and going up to the room. As she had expected, Valerie was already there and clearly sound asleep. Carmen crept in as quietly as possible and without putting on the light. She put her bag down beside the empty bed and felt her way to the bathroom where she turned on the light and left the door open just a crack. Enough to see what she was doing, but not enough to wake Valerie. She changed quietly into her pyjamas, turned out the bathroom light and climbed into bed. After two tiring days, it was not hard to get to sleep.

Vincent awoke early. He looked at the red glow of figures on the bedside clock. Not quite six o'clock and dawn was starting to show through a gap in the window drapes. A long sleep, he thought, but at least he felt refreshed and not as if he was starting flu. A shower and breakfast should complete the revival. He climbed out of bed and opened the drapes just enough to look through. There wasn't much to see from the sixth floor except a distant New Jersey across the Hudson River, as it was still fairly dark. He turned and went into the bathroom, not noticing in the half light how the other bed was occupied.

Twenty minutes later, Carmen woke up. The bathroom light was on and she could have sworn there was a male voice singing as she woke up. Now all she could hear was the sound of someone brushing their teeth. She looked across the other bed at the clock showing the time in red digits. It was gone six o'clock. Time to get up and get busy. She swung her feet out of bed, turned on the bedside lamp and stretched, pushing her curly hair back off her face. As she did so, the bathroom door opened and a very large, very tall, very blond, very muscular and very naked man walked out, rubbing a bath towel on his head to dry his hair.

Carmen screamed.

Vincent froze and lifted the towel up from his face so he could see. To his complete shock there was a girl sitting on the other bed in pyjamas with wide eyes, a hand to her mouth and looking scared. His jaw dropped in surprise. He couldn't fail to notice that although she looked scared, she had beautifully proportioned Latin features, glossy jet black hair hanging down to her shoulders, curves in all the right places and she was probably the prettiest girl he had ever seen.

Carmen noticed his shock and surprise and so stopped screaming. He really didn't look like someone about to attack her, but who knows? And he still shouldn't be there.

"Get out of my room!" she shouted, looking around for something to throw at him.

"It's not your room, it's my room," he said in an annoyed voice, "and where did you come from?"

"No, it's *not* your room," said Carmen, "it's mine; at least it's mine and Valerie Kingsley's room. What are you doing here?"

As she said it, she noticed movement below his waist and her eyes couldn't help but drift downwards past a muscled chest and a six pack to the part of Vincent which was getting larger and larger. She drew in her breath suddenly, her eyes got even bigger and her hand covered her mouth again.

Vincent now realised he was wearing nothing but a damp towel on his head. He quickly took the towel off his head and tied it around his waist. Carmen's eyes flicked back to his face.

"Ah, I think I see the problem," said Vincent, thinking about what she had said and relaxing slightly. "I think there's been a misunderstanding. I'm Valerie's twin brother Vincent."

"Vincent? Vincent? Oh yes? Where's Valerie?" said Carmen, sounding cynical.

"Valerie couldn't come. She's got flu."

Suddenly, the truth of the matter became crystal clear to Carmen as well. The two V Kingsleys on the rooming list hadn't been a mistake, there really were two of them. Vincent and Valerie. Why hadn't someone told her? Why hadn't someone said which one wasn't coming? Why hadn't she asked why there were two names the same? What was Julia Wynne going to say if she found out about another Carmen Castro disaster? Carmen groaned, leaned forward and covered her face with both hands.

Vincent was still standing there holding his towel so it didn't slip, watching the emotions flicker across Carmen's face. He wasn't sure who this girl was, but it looked like a genuine mistake, not a suspicious trick of some sort.

Into the silent gap, as they both digested what had happened, came a pounding on the door.

"Hotel Security, open the door please."

Carmen and Valerie looked at each other in surprise.

Carmen realised she didn't want this new

blunder going any further and getting any bigger, so she quickly went to the door, put the security chain on and opened it a crack to see a security guard standing there.

"Are you ok ma'am? Only a maid heard a scream from this room."

"Oh, yes I'm fine," said Carmen, thinking quickly and improvising. "I just stubbed my toe on the furniture." She put her bare foot into the door opening by way of explanation.

The guard looked down and winced, even though the foot looked perfectly normal.

"Ow, it's painful when you do that! Are you sure you'll be ok. now?"

"Yes, it's feeling better already," lied Carmen, "thank you for your concern."

"Well good, ok, you have a nice day now," said the guard, waving his hand and turning to walk back down the hall.

"Thank you, bye," said Carmen, closing the door and turning to lean back on it with a sigh of relief.

Vincent had been watching this playacting with interest. He had found it particularly interesting to watch Carmen walking to the door and then turning to face him again. Pyjamas, even pink pyjamas printed with small fluffy sheep, didn't really provide much in the way of camouflage when you had curves like hers. As she hurried to the door, her backside and hips moved in a particularly rivetting way. Then as she turned to lean back against the door her breasts moved sideways under the pyjama top. Vincent couldn't tear his eyes away. If he had been thinking, then perhaps he would have thought it polite to look away, but just at the moment the only part of his body which wasn't functioning was his brain.

Carmen looked back at Vincent whose eyes were large, very blue and fixed on her. She forgot the security guard, as she realised she was still in a hotel bedroom and wearing very little. She was alone and there was a nearly naked large man looking intently at her. Should she have said something to the security guard? No. The situation was complicated enough already and she didn't really think her unexpected room mate was a threat. Not a physical threat perhaps, but possibly a threat to her sanity. Carmen looked back at him and felt a flush coming over her. Her pulse had been racing since the initial shock, but it didn't seem to be slowing at all. Her eyes took in his broad shoulders again and the size of his muscular biceps. As her eyes started to drift lower again, she did a sharp intake of breath as she noticed his towel seemed to be getting bigger at the front. However, despite the circumstances, it seemed he was here due to her mistake and not with some evil intent. Nevertheless, this was an embarrassing situation and she didn't want him getting any inappropriate ideas. Clearly she needed to get the situation onto some sort of business-like level before it got even more complicated. It was time for Carmen to take charge.

"Do you suppose we could get dressed before we try to sort this out?" she asked, pushing away from the door.

"Certainly," replied Vincent, as the question started him thinking again and he became conscious once more of the strange situation, "but perhaps you should face the wall while I put some clothes on?"

He wasn't shy, but neither did he want to be stared at while he got dressed. He also wanted to understand what was going on without being distracted.

"Oh, oh, of course."

Carmen hurried to her bed and sat on the side facing away from Vincent.

Vincent dropped the towel and starting getting clothes out of his suitcase.

"Now you know who I am, but I have no idea who you are."

"I'm Carmen Castro and I work for the publishing house. However, I've only been there a couple of months and didn't realise there were two of you. Two V Kingsleys that is," she continued, but mumbled, "and it's me who messed up the room assignments."

Vincent paused as he pulled on a pair of dark blue chinos.

"I'm sorry, I didn't quite hear the last bit, what did you say?"

Carmen answered, rather louder than really necessary, "It was me who messed up the room assignments. I thought you were Valerie. I didn't know there was a Vincent too. I'm sorry."

She paused for a moment.

"Why are there two of you? There's only one author isn't there?"

"Oh yes," said Vincent, shaking out a light blue

shirt, "and you can turn around now. Valerie, my twin sister, is the author and I'm her agent. We both meant to come, but she went down with flu the day before, so I came on my own. Your turn now," he said, buttoning up his shirt and indicating the bathroom with his head.

Carmen picked some clothes out of her bag and fled to the bathroom. Vincent tried not to watch her go past and failed miserably. As he heard the shower start he sat on the edge of the bed, putting on socks and shoes and wondering what else could go wrong on this trip.

Fifteen minutes later, after a shower, a fully dressed and contrite Carmen emerged from the bathroom to see Vincent sitting in an armchair watching the news on tv. He wasn't very interested in the local news, but there wasn't much else to do while waiting in a hotel room.

"Vincent ..., oh, is it ok if I call you Vincent?" she said, sitting in the other armchair.

He turned off the tv and turned to face her. A cream blouse and short tight grey skirt looked really good, even if they weren't quite as exciting as pyjamas with a fluffy sheep pattern. He pulled his thoughts back to her question and his eyes back to her face.

"Yes, yes, Vincent is fine. And did you say you were Carmen?"

"Yes, Carmen or CC," she said, nodding.

"Si, si?" he asked, feeling surprised, "do you always say 'yes' then?"

She laughed.

"No! C, C, my initials, Carmen Castro."

"Oh, right!" said Vincent, shaking his head and feeling a little stupid, "I'm sorry, I must be a little slow this morning what with the jet lag."

Carmen leaned forward, resting her elbows on her knees.

"Vincent, I've been thinking and I have to ask you a favour. This mix-up is all my fault and if my boss hears about this I'll be in big trouble. Do you suppose we can keep this quiet, and just between us, so nobody finds out about my blunder?"

Vincent shrugged. It wasn't the sort of thing he would be telling everyone about, it wouldn't be right. Even if it might be amusing with hindsight. Well, he might tell his sister, as it was kind of her fault, but definitely nobody else.

"Of course we can, I don't want you to get into trouble," he said reassuringly.

He also thought how if his contract was in danger, it might help to have someone on the inside who owed him a favour. Even though he didn't understand her position in the company at the moment.

Carmen pressed her lips together as she studied Vincent.

"I'm starving, how about we go for breakfast and talk about this?" suggested Vincent, slightly disconcerted by her gaze.

"Yes, fine, but lets keep this quiet, so a table for two away from everybody else?" said Carmen, standing up.

"Suits me," said Vincent, thinking he would like to keep it quiet too, because his situation with the publisher was already complicated enough. Who knew what the reaction would be when they found out Valerie, the supposed author, wasn't here?

"If anybody sees us they will think we are having a romantic breakfast on our own."

He smiled and waggled his eyebrows suggestively.

Carmen pursed her lips again and narrowed her eyes at him, before grabbing her bag and key and heading for the door.

Vincent sighed, wondering if his comment was a foolish mistake when they needed to co-operate. He already knew the American sense of humour was different from the British one, so he needed to be more careful with his remarks. He grabbed his key and wallet before following her to the door.

Chapter 4

They stood silently, side by side, waiting for the lift to arrive.

Vincent was thinking that if he had only known a girl as hot as CC was on the staff of the publisher, he might have turned up for the conference last year as well. It would have been worth taking a small chance on being discovered as the author rather than the agent as expected.

Carmen was replaying in her mind the scene as Vincent emerged from the bathroom. Now she was over the shock and surprise, she could consider his finer points. And some of them were very fine indeed. He was tall, broad shouldered and there wasn't an ounce of fat on him, just muscle. He wasn't heavy enough to be a body builder, but he obviously got plenty of exercise to have a six-pack like his. As well as the blonde hair on his head, he had a light covering of blond curly hair on his chest which went down to...

The bell of the lift dinged, interrupting the scene in her mind, the doors opened and they stepped inside. They turned to face the doors again, as Vincent pressed the button for the ground floor.

Carmen saw their muted reflection in the stainless steel lift doors and noticed she only came up to his shoulder. She turned and looked up at him. Vincent turned and looked back down at her.

"Exactly how tall are you?" she blurted out.

Vincent raised his eyebrows and Carmen felt slightly embarrassed.

"Six foot two," said Vincent, "how tall are you?"

"Five seven," replied Carmen and turned back to the doors in complete embarrassment as the lift came to a halt. Vincent said nothing, but Carmen could see a half grin in their reflection.

They picked a table in the corner, well away from the handful of other people in the restaurant. They ordered coffee from the waitress and then collected plates of food from the buffet.

Back at their table, Carmen, leant forward and whispered, "Vincent, I really do need you to keep it a secret about us sharing a room, otherwise I'm in big trouble."

Vincent froze for a moment.

"What is it?" he whispered back to her.

Just as he was wondering if he had found the girl of his dreams, he was now imagining a nightmare scenario of a husband bent on vengeance.

"You mean you're married?"

"Married!" exclaimed Carmen, waving her hands in front of her and struggling to keep her voice down.

"No, nothing like that. It's because if Julia Wynne finds out, she's bound to sack me for messing up the room assignments."

"Well that's a relief," said Vincent, saying the first thing which came into his head and forgetting to whisper.

He saw how Carmen suddenly looked dismayed.

Vincent realised he must have said the wrong thing and replayed the conversation in his head. He put his hand to his mouth, as he realised how it must have sounded. He went back to whispering.

"Oh, no, no, no, I am sorry, I didn't mean it would be a relief if you were sacked, it's the jetlag getting me muddled. I mean it's a relief I won't have an angry husband coming after me."

Vincent paused and realised he could be digging the hole he was in even deeper, if he wasn't very careful.

"Um, what I really mean is, surely not? It's just a simple mistake and easily fixed. One of us changes room this morning, we don't say anything and that's an end of it. She's not going to fire you over some simple easily understandable mistake and in any case, nobody will know but us."

Carmen grimaced.

"It's not quite so simple," she said quietly. "For a start, there are no more rooms. I should know, after all, I did the rooming list. Secondly, it's not one simple mistake, it's the latest in a whole series. I think Julia sent me here not just to help when we're shorthanded, but also to redeem myself."

Vincent was intrigued.

"A whole series of mistakes? What sort of mistakes?"

"I can't tell you, it's too humiliating, you just have to believe me," said Carmen, blushing again and becoming very interested in the food on her plate.

Vincent then realised what else she had said.

"No more rooms? You are suggesting we

continue to share?"

"What else can we do?"

Carmen suddenly looked worried and her eyes widened.

"You're not married yourself are you?"

"Oh no, I share a house with my twin Valerie, mostly because it's convenient and it keeps the cost down for both of us, but no, neither of us is married."

Carmen felt a sense of relief and realised she glad he was single. In fact, she thought, she was more than glad, she was pleased and excited too. She took a long look at him. It had been a while since she had met anyone quite as good looking as this and to whom she was attracted.

"Well, it's ok then," she said, carefully keeping her voice level, "provided you promise to keep to your side and I keep to my side. You'll have to be discrete too, because if anybody finds out, my career is dead in the water. You're sure you'll do this for me?"

She put her hand over Vincent's hand and looked into his eyes, trying to look as appealing as possible.

Vincent knew when she looked like this, he was putty in her hands, but he wasn't going to admit it.

"I'll do it on one condition," he said, determinedly looking stern, but turning his hand over and gently rubbing the back of her hand with his thumb.

"You have to tell me about the series of mistakes."

"You are an evil man," said Carmen, as she straightened up, saw what he was doing and jerked her hand away.

Vincent just grinned.

"Ok," said Carmen, "I will tell you, but only if you promise to help me. Promise?"

Vincent nodded, feeling pleased. He hoped the story of multiple mistakes would be entertaining and a way to tease her.

Chapter 5

After breakfast, Carmen went off to find
Elizabeth and see what was needed.

Vincent walked slowly back to the lifts in a
thoughtful state of mind. A couple of weeks ago he
could not have imagined his trip starting like this.
He still had to deal with a publisher who was
expecting to see his sister, who should have been
here, masquerading as the author Valerie Kay. If
they still insisted on a face-to-face meeting with the
supposed author, it would have to be later when
Valerie was over the flu. Hopefully they would not be
difficult, because the books had been selling well. In
the meantime, he would look forward to meeting the
delectable Carmen again and hearing the anecdotes
about more of her mistakes. She seemed smart so
far, so was she just unlucky or was she really scatter-
brained?

He went back to his room and called Valerie to
see how she was coping with her flu and to know if
their mother had arrived to help her. Vincent
decided not to mention Carmen. The situation
would seem improbable and she would be much
easier to explain when Vincent and Valerie were
face-to-face. And even then, he wasn't sure he
wanted it mentioned at all to his mother. Who knew
what her reaction would be? She might be
scandalised or might just see it as another
opportunity for heavy hints to both Vincent and
Valerie about the virtues of marriage. Either way, he
thought, it was best avoided.

Satisfied Valerie was being looked after, and

after a snack lunch, he went to the main conference room where the first business of the conference was about to start. It was a closed meeting for the publishing house to tell the authors and agents how business was going. This was to be followed by a question and answer session, before the general public arrived the next day.

Vincent entered the room just before the meeting was about to start and went to take a seat several rows back.

"Sir! Sir! Excuse me!" called out Julia Wynne from the table at the front of the room.

Vincent stopped and turned to her. He pointed to his chest, miming, 'me?'

"Yes, you sir, I'm sorry, but this is a private meeting for authors and agents only, I must ask you to leave," said Julia, pointing to the door.

Vincent put his hands out, palms up "but I *am* an agent, I'm Vincent Kingsley."

Julia glowered, she had obviously expected Valerie to be there, not Vincent, and she didn't look at all pleased. She clasped her hands and leant forward with a
frown.

"I was told you had flu and were not coming. I'm expecting Valerie Kingsley, where is she?"

"She is the one with flu and is at home in bed. I'm afraid you've just got me."

He smiled and just stood there, not moving. He knew Julia didn't like him, but she did like the books. Although there was a chance she wouldn't take another book from him, he had realised on the way over the Atlantic, his books had been selling well. He had earned out his advance a while ago. The publisher would undoubtedly want him to sign a fresh contract, it was more a question of what terms they would offer him. Valerie Kay's website was getting a steady trickle of visitors too and he was sure his next book would also sell well. There were surely other publishers who would be interested in signing an author with such a good track record. He was in a good bargaining position. So he was going to be polite but he wasn't going to be crawling to her either.

"Very well, please take a seat," said Julia, sounding annoyed there was nothing more she could say to get rid of him.

Vincent noticed Carmen was standing to the side, looking a little speculatively at her boss. He supposed Carmen hadn't been aware of Julia's antagonism towards the presence of men in their business.

"Let's get started," said Julia. "You should all have an annual update handout showing changes to personnel, performance during the year and ...."

She tailed off as she could see a lot people puzzled, looking around, shaking their heads.

Julia turned to her youngest assistant.

"Carmen, where are the handouts?"

Carmen shook her head.

"I don't know, I didn't know there were any."

Julia sighed impatiently.

On her other side, Elizabeth looked around her.

"Oh, here they are, stacked against the back wall. Carmen, help me hand these out. I'll do this side and you do the other."

Julia didn't look best pleased with the delay, but could do little except wait, drumming her fingers on the table while they were distributed. Elizabeth and Carmen both picked up a small stack of the glossy handouts and moved to the ends of the rows of chairs to hand them out. As Carmen leaned forward to pass some into a row across some empty chairs, the whole stack she was holding slid out of her grasp and cascaded under and over three rows of chairs. Cries of dismay from these rows were soon followed by a handful of ladies down on their knees helping to retrieve the handouts and pass them back to a red-faced Carmen.

Julia Wynne angrily rolled her eyes to the ceiling, shook her head and rested forward on her elbows, fiddling impatiently with a pen while she waited for order to be restored.

Meanwhile, Vincent was sitting on the other side of the room watching everything with interest, whilst holding a handout given to him by Elizabeth. Was this the sort of thing Carmen was referring to? He rubbed the handout with a couple of fingers. It was glossy and slippery, so it wasn't surprising if a stack should slip onto the floor. If your boss was glaring at you impatiently and you were in a hurry too, a minor accident like this was entirely understandable. Julia's attitude was unhelpful, to say the least.

Come the coffee break, Vincent stood casually next to Carmen, half facing each other as if they had only just met.

Carmen said quietly, "Does Julia not like you?"

"No, I think she believes men don't belong here. She doesn't look too keen on you either," he replied, also keeping his voice down.

"No, well, it's not surprising when I'm so clumsy. I just hope nothing else goes wrong."

"It wasn't so bad. Nothing broke. It wasn't a public meeting, I expect it will soon be forgotten."

Carmen wasn't so sure, but decided to ignore it and think positively. Here she was, standing next to a guy she was finding hugely attractive and whom she would definitely like to know better. In two days they would be going in opposite directions. If she wanted to become more than polite friends with him, it was no good waiting to see if something would happen. She needed to act and make something happen. If he pushed her away, it would be too bad, but at least she wouldn't be kicking herself for doing nothing. She looked up and turned to face him a little more.

"I hope so. Listen, are you going to take dinner with me this evening?" asked Carmen hopefully.

Vincent hesitated.

"As much as I would love to, I don't think it's a good idea. Firstly, we don't want to attract attention, and secondly I've got jetlag. I'll probably grab a sandwich and have another early night. Also, this way, if we're not seen together, nobody will notice which rooms we have."

He was right, but Carmen admitted to herself that she was disappointed, her shoulders dropped and she sighed gently.

"Yes, you're right. Leave the bathroom light on so I can see when I get there and don't disturb you, ok?"

Vincent nodded and turned to be introduced to Elizabeth who had just walked up.

Elizabeth had noticed Carmen's body language and she guessed an invitation of some sort had just been turned down. Elizabeth looked carefully at them both, but couldn't guess exactly what had been said. She was left speculating about what it might have been. Given that Vincent was not only a good looking guy but the only man there, apart from hotel staff, it was no great strain on the imagination to think of something. Elizabeth was left wondering if Carmen had a sufficiently appropriate professional attitude.

Chapter 6

Saturday in New York. The day when the general public could attend. The bedside alarm went off. Carmen sleepily stretched out a hand to switch it off. She groped around and couldn't find the clock but it stopped anyway.

A male voice said, "Good morning," and she was suddenly wide awake. Remembering the previous morning, she peeped out from under the covers.

"Don't worry, I'm wearing pyjamas this morning," said Vincent, "I'll take a shower and then you can have your turn."

He picked up some clothes and headed to the bathroom. Carmen sank back onto the pillow. She wasn't sure if she should be relieved or disappointed. On the one hand he was being a gentleman and not, as they say, 'forcing his attentions on her' was he? On the other hand, maybe he didn't find her attractive. He had refused dinner with her yesterday as well. This wasn't a problem she normally had, but a man this good looking could probably pick and choose from the prettiest girls around. However, she mused, his physical reaction to her yesterday morning had been pretty quick and rather obvious, so he couldn't be finding her totally unattractive could he? Maybe he liked her body but found her personality repulsive? She couldn't guess what he was thinking and it was very confusing.

Ho hum, she thought, as she lay back and looked up at the ceiling. It was going to be a busy day today, so not being distracted by a dishy guy was probably a good thing. She really needed to concentrate on keeping her job. Next week he would be gone back to England, but hopefully she would still have her job in California. It was important to stay on the right side of Julia.

She listened to him singing in the shower. A Jennifer Lopez track sung by a man didn't sound right, especially when his Spanish accent was abysmal. But all the same, listening to a man singing in your shower was an interesting novelty. Before long he emerged from the bathroom clean, shaved and dressed.

"Your turn," he said.

"I'll go straight down to breakfast and see you there, so people don't see us leaving the room together."

Carmen realised he was definitely keeping his distance. It was all very well and proper, but she wanted to get to know him so much better and this was frustrating. She waited for him to leave before getting out of bed and heading for the shower.

When she got down to the restaurant, there was no chance of joining him. He was seated at a large table which was full of ladies. There was plenty of space at other tables, but not at his. Carmen felt a spurt of annoyance as she found a spare seat next to Elizabeth.

"He's got plenty of company this morning, hasn't he?" Carmen said to Elizabeth, nodding in the direction of Vincent.

"It's not really surprising is it? I mean, as much as I love my husband, he wasn't as good looking as

Vincent when I married him twenty five years ago."

She took a reflective sip of coffee.

"Since those ladies all read romance, they're probably all of a romantic disposition. Then they come down to breakfast having left any husbands or boyfriends at home and this blond god appears amongst them. As they're probably all readers of his sister's books, he's got to be at least polite to them, hasn't he?"

"I suppose so," said Carmen, unable to keep a little irritation out of our her voice, "I hope they leave him room to breathe."

Carmen noticed Elizabeth looking at her speculatively, before continuing to drink her coffee. She would have to mind what she said or did if she was not to give the game away. As she ate her breakfast she wondered why she was annoyed. She thought she and Vincent had found an instant rapport and were friends weren't they? However, she had no particular claim on Vincent, nor him on her, beyond an instant friendship and a shared secret did they? Maybe he didn't feel particularly friendly towards her, because he was certainly keeping away from her. Carmen sat quietly analysing her feelings. Maybe it was just her competitive streak and jealousy? She looked again at the group crowding around Vincent. At least half of them were old enough to be his mother, she thought grumpily. She then shrugged and concentrated on her breakfast. Maybe she could take coffee with him later.

"This morning," said Elizabeth to Carmen, once they had both finished eating, "there's the welcome speech by Julia and then the keynote address by one of the editors. This time it's about the impact of e-publishing, followed by questions and answers. We need to be there for the welcome by Julia, and then we go next door to finish setting up for the book signing session in the afternoon."

"What about Valerie Kay?" asked Carmen, "do we just stack her books on a table for people to pick up since she's not here to sign them?"

"I thought of asking Vincent to sit there," replied Elizabeth, glancing thoughtfully at the other table, where Vincent was still surrounded by his female fans. "It's not the same, but he's her brother as well as her agent, so I thought people might like to ask him about her."

"Good idea," said Carmen, determinedly not looking at the other table, "shall we go and set up for the morning talks? I'll ask Vincent about the book signing if he ever gets away from those ladies."

She couldn't help herself and looked across to where Vincent was hemmed in by his admirers, as she stood and followed Elizabeth out of the hotel restaurant.

Chapter 7

Everything was ready for the welcome speech. Julia and her four senior editors were seated at the table on the dais facing the audience, the last of whom were trickling in to the rows of chairs at the back. A laptop computer was open on the table in front of Julia with her presentation ready to start. The title page was being displayed from a projector onto the screen above and behind Julia. Carmen and Elizabeth were standing to the side, ready to close the doors and dim the lights.

Julia took a sip of water and cleared her throat, ready to start as soon as the last people sat down. As she did so, she looked down at a low battery warning light flashing on the computer and, looking around, saw the charger was not plugged in.

"Psst!"

She beckoned Carmen to come over. Carmen hurried over, eager to help and unable to think of anything which might have gone wrong.

"Plug my charger into the wall socket over there," said Julia, holding the plug and pointing to the socket on the wall behind her.

Carmen took the plug and quickly went to put it into the wall socket. Unfortunately she didn't notice that it was several inches too short, so as she went to plug it in, she pulled the laptop across the table. It in turn pulled the projector, so the image was now displayed in a distorted form on the side wall of the room. Then, as the laptop went sliding across the table, the lid closed and so the distorted image now showed 'Microsoft Windows shutting down' on a blue background.

Julia screeched and grabbed in vain for the laptop as it went past her. The nearest editor grabbed the projector to stop it going any further and cursed as she put a hand on the hot bulb cover. Carmen turned around to see what was happening. Her eyes opened wide and her mouth dropped open in horror at the sudden chaos. What had she done now? The large audience had their attention gripped by the unexpected entertainment.

Julia opened the laptop once more and started arranging everything back to where it should be on the table. Elizabeth bustled up with a power cord extension cable in her hand to connect the charger to the wall socket. While the computer was starting up again, Julia turned angrily to Carmen.

"Get out of my sight," she hissed at her.

Elizabeth looked at the expression on Julia's face, turned Carmen towards the door and gave her a gentle push before kneeling down to reconnect the charger with the longer power cord.

Carmen pressed her lips together and headed for the door, trying not to cry and trying not to run.

As soon as the presentation started and the lights were dimmed, Vincent slipped out of the room by another door at the back, which was nearer to his row of chairs.

He found Carmen next door in the book signing room. She was standing just inside, holding a tissue to her eyes. He said nothing, but put his arms around her shoulders and pulled her towards him.

She looked up, saw it was Vincent, rested her forehead on his shoulder and put her arms around his waist. Carmen felt miserable. This was her first job and she so wanted everything to go right, but everything kept going wrong, time after time. It was nice to have someone to lean on, but by Tuesday he would be gone and she would be back at her desk and on her own again. At least, she hoped she would be back at her desk. She shuddered a little as she took a deep breath and straightened up. She took her arms from Vincent's waist, stepping back slightly and dabbing her eyes with the tissue. She looked at Vincent's shirt where there was now a large wet patch.

"I'm so sorry, I've made your shirt wet," she said, lifting her red eyes up to his face.

Vincent pulled her forward again, kissed her forehead and set her back once more.

"It doesn't matter, it's just a shirt, it'll soon dry."

He took a clean handkerchief from his pocket and offered it to her.

"Blow your nose, go to the ladies room and splash some cold water on your face, then come back and tell me about this book signing."

Carmen nodded, grateful for the comforting embrace and a suggestion of something simple to do, because she couldn't think straight at the moment. She blew her nose and left in search of the ladies room.

When she had gone, Vincent put his hands in his pockets and looked around. There were tables arranged around the outside of the room, each with a chair and several cardboard boxes. Inspection of the nearest stack of boxes revealed it was full of books and he took one out to read the dustcover. It was by an author he didn't know, but it sounded intriguing. It was tempting to get a copy to take home, but with a moment's reflection he realised he couldn't. He would probably want copies of all the other books too and his baggage weight limit for the flight home wouldn't allow it. He reluctantly put the book back into the box.

The door opened and Carmen re-appeared. She offered him his handkerchief with a small smile.

"Thank you, I'm feeling a bit better now."

"You keep it, I have more," he said, waving back her offer of the handkerchief.

Carmen hesitated, looking down at the tiny pockets of her business suit.

"I can't, it's too big for my pockets."

She offered it to him again and this time he took it and put it back in his own pocket.

"Ok, so tell me about this book signing. Valerie's not here, so what do we do with her books which I am supposing are here somewhere."

He waved an arm around the room at all the tables and boxes.

"Well," said Carmen, "the entrance ticket includes five free books and a bag to carry them, but quantities are limited. If they have a strong preference, they have to make sure they get to the front of an author's line before the author runs out of books. When they get given a book, the author puts a check mark in one of the five spaces on their ticket to make sure they don't get greedy and take more than five. Elizabeth and I wondered if you would mind sitting at Valerie's table and talking to her readers? After all, you know her books and you know Valerie pretty well, considering that you're her twin brother and agent too. The readers are getting a free book, so even if it's not signed, hopefully they won't mind too much."

Vincent thought that since it was him who had written the books, he knew 'Valerie's' books a lot better than he could admit. Then, descriptions of 'Valerie' would need some careful editing and adjustment, to combine the real person with his writing, if he was not to give himself away.

"Why don't we offer them some pre-signed books?" he asked.

"Simple. We don't have any!" replied Carmen.

"Ah! But we could you know. I can do her signature just as well as she can do mine. We're twins and we learnt to do it years ago. It's been convenient now and again."

"I'm not sure it would be right," said Carmen doubtfully.

Vincent, of course, knew it would be perfectly correct, even if it looked wrong, so he wasn't troubled by the idea.

"We can pre-sign a few and then offer people the choice: blank or pre-signed. They might be slightly disappointed the way the book isn't signed to include their name, but as you say, they're getting a free book anyway. Either way they're going to be happy."

Carmen chewed her lip. She was not entirely convinced, but she could see his point and Vincent was, in any case, Valerie's twin, not someone totally unconnected with the author.

"Alright, lets do it," she decided impulsively, letting out a large breath, "but you have to do it now while everybody is still next door. If anybody comes in, I'll deny all knowledge of it, otherwise I'll be completely sunk. I'm in enough trouble already. Let's find her books. You go that way around the room and I'll go this way."

They circled the room, checking the contents of the boxes until they found the books by Valerie Kay in one of the far corners. Carmen started taking books from the boxes and stacking them on one side of the table. Vincent signed them as 'Valerie Kay' and then put them on the other side for Carmen to replace in the boxes.

Vincent had just finished and stood up, when the door opened and Elizabeth came in.

Carmen went over to her, trying to look innocent.

"Vincent was helping me check that Valerie's book were delivered," she improvised, not very well, "and he's happy to sit at the table later and hand the books out."

Carmen looked at Elizabeth who raised an eyebrow, looked from Carmen to Vincent and back again.

Carmen waited for a cynical question about what had they really been doing. However, Elizabeth just gave a tiny shrug as if it didn't matter what, exactly, they had been doing. Carmen let out the breath she was holding. She didn't really mind if Elizabeth thought they had been doing something more personal. After all, it wasn't so very far from the truth, was it?

Vincent came over and smiled at Elizabeth.
"Now you're here, I'll go back and listen to the keynote speeches."
Elizabeth looked at him hard for a moment before saying "thank you for helping Carmen, we'll see you later on."
He looked Elizabeth in the eye, nodded understanding and went back to the room next door.

Elizabeth turned to Carmen.
"Let's not dwell on the earlier incident. You'll need to help me now to get all the books out on the tables before lunch, ready for later. If we're quick, we'll have time for a sandwich before everybody comes in. Then you can help me keep it all organised and sort out any problems which arise."

Chapter 8

Lunchtime was past and the book signing room was busy. Elizabeth and Carmen stood near the door surveying the activity, alert for any assistance which might be needed. Every table had a line of ladies in front of it holding a bag of books and waiting for a moment with the author as a book was signed for them. There was a loud buzz of conversation in the room.

"I wasn't sure what would happen with Valerie Kay not being here and her agent sitting at the desk," remarked Carmen, " but it seems to be working out fine."

"More than fine. Haven't you noticed he has the longest line in the room?"

Carmen glanced around the room and looked again at Vincent's table.

"You're right, I hadn't realised, maybe those pre-signed books did the trick."

"Pre-signed books?" queried Elizabeth. "Those books came straight from the printers."

Carmen looked away and wondered what to say.

"I think you've misunderstood," continued Elizabeth, "if you look, you can see he's writing in each book."

"He is? He can't do that if he's not the author can he?" protested Carmen, conveniently forgetting their earlier activity.

"You watch," said Elizabeth.

"See, next lady arrives at the table. He gives them an electric smile and takes a book from the stack."

Elizabeth couldn't help a small sigh at the smile.

"Then he listens to what they want written in the book. Ooh! That must be a saucy one, he looked a bit shocked for a moment there, but he's writing it anyway."

"Saucy? What do you mean saucy?" asked a puzzled Carmen.

"Well the last time I went over there to see if he wanted a coffee, I looked over his shoulder and he was writing 'think of me when you are reading this in bed. Vincent Kingsley'. He didn't even look embarrassed at that one."

"What? Can he do that? I mean he's not even the author! Is he allowed to?" said Carmen in alarm.

"I think he's writing whatever they ask him to and I'm not going to stop him. He can always suggest some other inscription if they cross the line too far. Now look! He's finished that book and she's handed her camera to the next person in line to take a photo. He stands beside her, she puts his arm across her shoulders and oh!.. Do you know, from the expression on his face and her missing right hand, I think she just grabbed his butt!"

"It's too much! I'm going over there," said Carmen crossly.

Elizabeth grabbed her arm.

"No, wait! We don't want a scene. I think he's coping with it. Now watch, he looks around the room to see where you are and sits down to greet the next one."

"What do you mean, he's looks around to see where I am?" asked a bewildered Carmen.

"Every time," said a smug Elizabeth, "I'm not

even sure if he knows he is doing it. He doesn't call you over, so I think he just needs to know where you are."

Carmen watched Vincent deal with another reader and Elizabeth was right. He was concentrating on the book signing and wasn't lingering when he saw Carmen, but he was definitely checking to see where she was.

Elizabeth put a hand on Carmen's shoulder.

"CC, go and ask him quietly if he needs any coffee or maybe an armed guard."

Carmen glanced at Elizabeth and wondered what she was thinking, before she headed across the room and behind Vincent's table.

"Vincent, could I interrupt you for a moment please?" she said over his shoulder.

"Of course. Ladies, would you excuse me for just one moment?" he said, putting a finger in the air, smiling at the line in front of him and standing.

He turned to partly face the wall and said very quietly, "you have to save me!"

"What? How? Now?" whispered Carmen, wondering what on earth she could or should do.

"No, no, later!" said Vincent urgently, "you would not believe how many invitations to dinner...and... and other invitations I'm getting here."

Carmen's eyes widened, "what shall I do?"

"Each time I have to tell them I'm sorry, but I regret how I can't join them later because I'm having dinner with Valerie's editor and I couldn't possibly change that."

"But she's sick, she's not here, she's at home in

California," said a puzzled Carmen.

"No, no, she's standing right here. For today you're the editor. Got it?"

"Oh... right," said Carmen as the light dawned.

She turned partly back towards the room and raised her voice, "that's excellent, I'll see you at dinner."

She squeezed his arm and looked him in the eye.

"Good, good, see you later," he replied with a quick smile and sat again at the table.

Carmen glanced at the book he was in the middle of writing. It said 'dear Delia, we must stop meeting like this at conferences, people will talk. Vincent.'

Carmen shrugged. Presumably this was one to be shown to friends, complete with a photo, to make them jealous. She headed back to Elizabeth.

Just as Carmen got there, Julia came into the room. She gave Carmen a sour look and asked Elizabeth how it was going. Elizabeth said everything was fine and mischievously added that Vincent was doing a great job with Valerie's books. Julia looked across at Vincent.

"But he's signing books," she hissed, "he can't do that!"

"He *is* doing it and the *customers* are loving it, so I decided to leave well alone."

Julia stood there with a face like thunder, watching what was going on and debating what to do.

"Fine!" she snapped, "it's up to you and I don't want to know about it."

She turned abruptly and left the room.

Chapter 9

The book signing finished, Vincent went up to his room to freshen up, while Carmen stayed behind to help Elizabeth clear the room. Half an hour later, Carmen went up to their room to find Vincent fully dressed and sound asleep on his bed.

"Wake up, sleepyhead," she said, "it's time to go eat."

He didn't move.

She sat on the side of his bed and shook his shoulder but he just snorted a little and carried on sleeping. Carmen studied him for a few moments more and then gave in to the temptation which she realised she had had for quite a while. She bent down and kissed him lightly on the lips. At first he didn't react, but then his eyes popped open and his arms came around her to pull her down and deepen it into an open mouthed kiss. After a few minutes she eased up onto her elbows so she could speak.

"Time to wake up Prince Charming!"

Vincent grinned up at her.

"It was just a little jetlag nap, but I'm definitely awake now Princess ... What was her name?"

He frowned in thought.

Carmen studied his face at very close range.

"Depending on the version, it was either Aurora, Rosamond or Rosebud. I think Disney used Aurora."

"Not Carmen?" he said, and brushed his lips across hers.

"No, definitely not Carmen."

She leaned forward to rest a little on his chest.

"You are remarkably well informed on a slightly

obscure topic. Where did you learn this?"

"Stanford. I majored in English Literature and it turned up in one of the options. I was always partial to fairy tales."

"Hmm. I read English at Cambridge but it had nothing as exciting as that."

"Were you and Valerie on the same course?"

"No, we were at the same college, but she did Biochemistry."

"Biochemistry? And now she's the author and you're the agent?"

Vincent realised he had been distracted, careless and nearly let the cat out of the bag. Hardly surprising when he was still a little sleepy, a pretty girl was almost laying on top of him and her face was only an inch away. If she moved any further onto him it wouldn't be the only revelation either. There had been no doubt about his attraction to her since the first morning, but he had been holding back. Accusations of assault were a scenario he didn't need, especially in a foreign country and with an employee of his publisher. However, since she had made the first move, it seemed unlikely the scenario would arise. But in any case, he would still need to tread carefully to avoid a difficult situation. Perhaps it was time to change the subject, as much as he was reluctant to end this interesting interlude.

"It's funny how things turn out sometimes. How long have I been asleep?"

Carmen looked at the bedside clock.

"About half an hour. Time to freshen up and get something to eat before the dance."

She sat up.

"Dance? I don't recall anything about a dance. What kind of dance?"

"Line dancing. Are you coming with me?"

Vincent groaned.

"You don't like line dancing?"

"I've tried it, but it's not really to my taste. My idea of dancing is with a partner and something like Salsa."

"Oh, that's much more cool, I love Salsa but it's never going to work with a hundred women and one man is it?"

"No, I suppose not," said Vincent in resignation.

"Since it's you asking, I'll go, but only if you have dinner with me as Valerie's editor, like we said, and then you promise to be my bodyguard for the evening."

Carmen put her hands on his chest and narrowed her eyes.

"Oh, I think I can manage it."

She caressed the muscles of his chest through the fine material of his shirt for a moment, then realised this might not be the best idea. The whole situation was already complicated. She was in enough trouble at this point, without getting involved with one of their authors. He was very tempting, but it was unprofessional of her, wasn't it? She stood up and sprang away before he could pull her down again.

"But my turn first in the shower this time."

Chapter 10

Vincent went into the ballroom with some trepidation. Among the Stetsons, fringed shirts and cowboy boots he felt rather under-dressed. He gave Carmen a resigned look. She had come prepared with embossed boots, very tight jeans and a white embroidered and sleeveless top. A red, white and blue bandana and a red cowboy hat which had CC in gold letters on the front completed the look.

Carmen looked over the rest of the crowd, then pursed her lips and gave Vincent a considering look. He was wearing blue chinos with a plain white shirt. She took off her hat and put it on Vincent's head. She stood back a little and looked at him.

"Better. Now lets go and join Elizabeth at the table over there."

Vincent adjusted the hat slightly. He wasn't sure if he felt more or less self-conscious now.

"So, CC, you're putting your label on me are you?"

"I certainly am. I'm your author's editor for the day, remember?"

Then she growled at him, "and tonight you're mine, so come on."

She headed across the room towards Elizabeth with a rather bemused Vincent following her. He wasn't quite sure how much to read into the last comment.

Carmen sat next to Elizabeth, leaned towards her and whispered in her ear.

"In the book signing room, he asked for

protection from the ladies besieging him. I'm pretending to be Valerie Kay's editor and therefore monopolising her agent."

Elizabeth listened carefully, her eyes flicked towards Vincent and she snorted before nodding agreement. She then leant across Carmen and put her hand on Vincent's arm to gain his attention.

"Vincent, we haven't had a chance to chat, so why don't you come and sit between Valerie's *editor* and me?"

Vincent and Carmen changed places.

Elizabeth leaned towards Vincent and said quietly, "this way you have a bodyguard both sides of you; otherwise you might get abducted."

She tipped her head to one side, indicating a table nearby.

Vincent glanced, as casually as he could, towards the table she indicated, as he pretended to look around the room. He was being scrutinised, fairly blatantly, by eight ladies sitting around the table. He looked back at Elizabeth and shivered slightly.

"Now I know how the fox feels when it hears the foxhounds baying."

"Come on you two," said Carmen, pulling at his arm as she stood up, "it's about to start."

The first line dance routine was fairly straightforward, so as to get everyone going. The three of them were more or less in the middle of the floor, so as they turned each time through 90 degrees, they were able to see the rest of the crowd. When Vincent found Carmen in front of him, he just couldn't look at the crowd beyond her. His entire focus was her curly black swaying hair, the excellence of her hip action and how her jeans were really rather tight across the back. He was glad his chinos were a comfortably loose, rather than tight, fit. Even so, he was still relieved that when the ladies were facing him, it was his back they were seeing, not his front. Very aware he was the only man in the room, he had no wish to incite added interest or, god forbid, any pointing at the area of his zip. It was just as well he didn't realise the interest of the ladies behind him, including Carmen, studying broad shoulders tapering down to a narrow waist and firm buttocks.

A couple of hours later, the three of them decided it was enough after a long day, and it was time to head for their beds. In the lift, Elizabeth asked which floor they wanted.

"Sixth please," said Vincent, and Carmen froze for a moment.

"How about that?" she said, trying hard to sound normal, "me too!"

Elizabeth didn't notice anything amiss and pressed the five button for her floor and the six button for theirs. Both Vincent and Carmen started breathing again. If Elizabeth had been on the same floor, how could they have avoided her realising they were sharing the same room?

Elizabeth got out on the fifth floor, saying to Carmen she would see her at eight in the morning for breakfast. The lift doors closed behind her and the lift started moving again. Vincent and Carmen looked at each other.

"That was close," said Carmen, "it would have been tricky if she'd been on the same floor as us."

"Very," replied Vincent, "I would have had to pretend I needed to go back to the lobby for something."

The lift stopped on their floor and they got out, looking both ways to make sure there was nobody else in sight. Then they ran down the hall, opened their door quickly and went inside before anybody could see them. They leant back against the wall and started laughing about it.

"Shh!" said Carmen, putting her hand over Vincent's mouth, "anybody passing will hear us and the game will be up!"

Vincent stopped laughing and kissed the palm of Carmen's hand instead. Their eyes locked and they moved together for the longer kiss which had been hanging between them since the last time they had been in the room.

Some time later, their heads moved apart slightly, so they could focus on each other's face.

Carmen said, "Do you suppose your bed is wide enough for two?"

Chapter 11

Sunday. Carmen awoke from where she had been sleeping comfortably on Vincent's chest. She glanced at the bedside clock which said eight o'clock. She pushed herself up to get a clearer view which produced an 'Oof!' from Vincent.

"I have to get dressed and get downstairs," she said, looking down at Vincent, "doesn't the alarm work?"

"It works fine," he replied, "but I seem to recall that we switched it off an hour ago and became distracted."

He started kneading her bottom which was conveniently placed under his hands.

"No, no, don't start again!" said Carmen, pushing his hands away and climbing out of bed.

"I need to shower quickly and get downstairs. And when I've finished you had better have a good shower if you don't want people smelling my perfume on you, which would be a real giveaway."

She looked at Vincent, lying back in bed with his hands behind his head and noticed the shape of the sheet which was covering him.

"It looks like it should be a cold shower too."

It was a day for appointments between editors, authors and agents. None of these were relevant for Vincent since he was pretending to be his own agent and his real editor had flu. In parallel there were a series of talks and workshops on a variety of subjects. By early afternoon, Vincent was sitting listening to Julia Wynne herself, speaking of lady's fashions in Regency times. He had taken a seat at the end of a row towards the back. This way he could sneak out if it became too boring, considering he didn't write historical fiction. Instead, a good lunch, a warm room, dim lights and some remaining jet lag were taking their toll. He was drifting off to sleep. At first, all was well, because the room was dim and nobody was looking his way. But then he started to snore and more than one person looked around to see who it was and giggle to their neighbour.

The disturbance caught the attention of Julia and she paused for a moment to see what was going on. Once she saw who it was, she had to keep her fury bottled up. Not only was someone sleeping during her talk, it was Vincent Kingsley who, in her opinion, simply didn't belong there anyway. She waggled her finger at Elizabeth indicating that she should do something about it, before resolutely turning and continuing with her talk.

Elizabeth was on the far side of the room from Vincent so she made signs to Carmen to go and wake Vincent.

Carmen went around to Vincent and hissed, "Vincent, Vincent," at him and poked him in the arm. It had no effect and Vincent slept on, dead to the world, as if he had been awake and busy nearly all last night instead of sleeping... Carmen pulled urgently at Vincent's sleeve.

Unfortunately, Vincent was just at the point where a person sleeping in a chair sometimes slumps forward and a tug on his sleeve was enough to send him sprawling on the floor. If this had not been enough to wake him, the cries of alarm from the ladies nearby would have been.

The interruption was enough to stop Julia speaking again and she glared in their direction. The pause in the speaking made Carmen look up to see a furious Julia pointing at the door. Vincent had got to his feet and Carmen grabbed his arm and pulled him from the room.

Out in the corridor, a flustered Carmen was brushing imaginary carpet dust off Vincent's chest and arms.

"I'm so sorry, I didn't mean to pull you onto the floor, but you were snoring and everyone was looking!

"A bit drastic, isn't it?" asked Vincent, "wouldn't telling me to wake up have been enough?"

"I tried that and it had no more effect than it did yesterday. You were well away in the Land of Nod"

"You could have tried the same method as yesterday; it worked pretty well then."

Carmen pulled a wry face and just looked at him.

"Yes well, not surprising I fell asleep I suppose," conceded Vincent, "Ladies Fashions in The Regency are a bit boring for a guy who doesn't write historical novels."

Carmen thought his choice of phrase seemed a little odd, since he wasn't a writer of novels was he? Never mind historical romance novels. So she dismissed the idea.

"Why not go to your room and take a nap so you'll be fresh for the Presentation Dinner," she suggested.

Vincent looked thoughtfully at Carmen.

"I think it is a very sensible notion," he declared in a serious voice, "but I'm half asleep and I think you might have to help me find my room."

Carmen put her most serious face on.

"Of course I will. We wouldn't want someone to stumble across you asleep in the hall, would we? I'll come with you and make sure you are properly tucked in."

She couldn't help waggling her eyebrows at him as he had done to her on Friday morning.

Chapter 12

Carmen was half asleep slumped across Vincent's chest again. Vincent was running his fingers through her hair and then down her back.

"Where do you live exactly?" he asked.

"Santa Monica," she said to his chest, "I share an apartment on South Barrington Avenue with a couple of girl friends."

"Do you work in Santa Monica too?"

"No, I work in LA, but it's only thirty minutes on the bus."

"Sounds like it might not be too far from the airport either," he said thoughtfully.

"No, it's just over an hour in the other direction on the bus. What about you? Where do you live?"

"I live in Murray Road, Wimbledon, in south west London. I share a house with my sister Valerie. It's very convenient. Not far from the station for her and not far from the common either."

"What's the common?"

"It's a big park. It's so big it's like being in the countryside, there's even a windmill."

"It sounds nice," said Carmen wistfully, "is this the Wimbledon where they play the tennis tournament?"

"Yes, it's the same Wimbledon. The tennis is at the big tennis club, not on the common, but it's not far away either."

Carmen tried to imagine the area and what it would be like to visit.

"Is it far from the airport?"

"No," said Vincent, "it's about an hour on the

tube from Heathrow airport."

"The tube?"

"The underground railway."

Carmen lay there, snuggled comfortably against Vincent, thinking about what he had just told her.

"What did you mean," she said, "when you said the station is convenient for your sister?"

Vincent realised the cat would get completely out of the bag sooner or later, so maybe this was the time to confess.

"Can you keep a secret?" he asked.

"I think we've been doing pretty well the last couple of days. What's your secret?"

"The truth is, I write as Valerie Kay and my sister Valerie is my agent. Which is to say that I'm the author and my sister is the agent, not me. A part time agent when she's not working at her full time job as a biochemist."

He felt Carmen go still as she absorbed and puzzled it out. "That's why you said she was a biochemist. She's not an author? You swapped identities? But why?"

Vincent sighed.

"Because it's a well known scientific fact that men don't read romantic fiction, and they certainly don't write it, do they? Everybody thinks all the readers are women too. So people raise their eyebrows at men who admit to reading it. I have no doubt many men won't admit it because they don't want to seem effeminate. Consequently I suspect there are actually more male readers than people realise. After all, if you're reading a book on an ereader, nobody can see the cover of the book and know you're reading romance. Anyway, I couldn't get published as a male writer, so my sister and I swapped identities. Once the book was by Valerie Kay, presumably female, I managed to get published. I mean to say, Julia gets her knickers in a twist when she thinks I'm just the agent for a female author who writes it. If she knew the truth, she wouldn't buy another book from me and she would probably go completely ape."

"What are knickers?"

"Female underwear. Panties?"

Carmen rolled onto her back and burst into uncontrolled laughter and Vincent couldn't help but join in.

"It's a brilliant joke on Julia," she said, "you should put it in one of your books."

"In the meantime my dear," said Vincent, kissing the tears of laughter from her cheeks, "we should get up, get dressed and go down to the dinner before we are missed."

"I expect we've already been missed, but people probably just think we're hiding from Julia after the fiasco this afternoon," said Carmen, sobering up, "and I wonder if Carmen's cooked goose is on the menu tonight."

A short while later they stood side-by-side in the bathroom, Vincent wearing another crisp white shirt and putting on a neck tie. Carmen was leaning towards the mirror putting on some vivid red lipstick which contrasted with her dark hair, eyebrows and eyelashes. She was wearing a plain matching red salsa dress which hugged her curves and left her shoulders bare. His tie done, Vincent moved behind her, pressed against her bottom and massaged her shoulders with his hands. She wriggled her bottom against him and turned around to face him. She put her arms around him and pulled him down for a quick kiss and his hands went around to knead her bottom.

"Vincent! Stop, stop or we'll never get downstairs," she said laughing.

She looked at his face, grabbed a tissue from the box on the counter and wiped the lipstick from his lips.

"There, go and put your jacket on," she said, before turning to see if her lipstick was messed up as well.

Vincent was enjoying this domesticity. It wasn't just the sex, good though it was, but there was a feeling of completion. It was as if there had been a piece of him missing which he had now found. Having Carmen for company was making him warm inside, in a way which was quite different from having a sister for company. He put his jacket on slowly as he analysed his feelings. Could it happen so fast? Could he be in love with this girl already?

Carmen emerged from the bathroom and picked up her shoulder bag. She stood in front of Vincent and looked up at him, smoothing his jacket over his shoulders and straightening his tie thoughtfully. Vincent looked down at her, wondering if she was feeling the same as him. She paused, then smiled brightly up at him. Too brightly perhaps.

"Come on," she said, "it's time to go."

Chapter 13

They arrived in the ballroom together to find it set out with round tables arranged for a formal dinner. The waiters were finishing off by putting the wineglasses out. At the entrance there was a chart on an easel of who was to sit on which table. Vincent found his table was at the back. He wasn't completely surprised and suspected that Julia had had an influence on the seating arrangements. Carmen was on a table near the front, as was Elizabeth, although on a different table on the other side of the room. More people were starting to trickle into the room and head for the seating list.

The dinner progressed smoothly and as the coffee was being served, Julia Wynne rose to her feet at the top table. She was smartly dressed in a cream cashmere suit with a white silk blouse and pearls. She posed and smiled as the official photographer took pictures. When the photographer was done, she took a couple of sheets of paper from the bag hanging on her chair. She was due to give some awards to various people and then make some closing remarks.

Vincent turned his chair so he could face the front as he drank his coffee. He watched as Julia looked around for the commemorative plaques for the awards and, not seeing them, beckoned Elizabeth over and asked her to get them.
There had been no room to store the plaques on or behind the top table, so they had been left in a

cardboard box in the corner of the room, just like the handouts previously. The plates had all been cleared away and so now there was space to stack the plaques on the table. Julia could then take them one by one from the table in front of her as she presented them to the winners. Elizabeth called Carmen to help her and they took the plaques from the box. They took a short stack each and went around the front, stepping up onto the podium in order to put the plaques on the table, just in front of Julia. As Carmen stretched forward to place her short stack of plaques next to those of Elizabeth, she was looking down to avoid tripping on the step. Thus she failed to notice the half full wine bottle which had been moved to the front of the table to make space. The bottom plaque clipped the top of the wine bottle, which then fell over and sprayed Julia with dark red wine.

There was a momentary hush as everybody at the top table saw what had happened. Elizabeth stood there with her hand to her mouth and her eyes wide with dismay. Carmen quickly put her plaques down and reached forward. As she righted the bottle, which was still spilling wine on the table, more wine flicked over Julia.

Julia stood there looking down in horror at the red wine splashes on her brand new outfit. Red wine on silk and cashmere was going to be impossible to remove. The second splash of wine made her look up slowly at Carmen, who was standing there, still holding the bottle. Horror changed to fury.

She leant forward and hissed at Carmen, "You are fired! Get out of my sight!"

Carmen turned and ran for the door. The audience went quiet as they realised there was a drama unfolding on the podium. They then erupted into noise with exclamations of dismay at the red splotches down Julia's front. Vincent stood up so he could see what was going on at the front of the room. He saw Carmen run out and quickly followed her, while other people were crowding to the front to get a better look.

"Clear this up, I have to change," said Julia to the others before she stomped off the platform.

Vincent caught up with Carmen at the lift. As they entered the lift, he saw Julia storming around a corner and he quickly pressed the button for their floor so the doors closed and Julia would have to take the other lift.

Carmen was sobbing her heart out and he pulled her to him without saying a word. He guided her to their room, sat in an armchair and pulled Carmen onto his lap. Vincent put his arms around her and let her cry. After a while the crying turned into sniffles and he handed her another one of his handkerchiefs.

He sat there in the chair holding her to him while she rested her head on his shoulder and put her hand on his chest, both of them deep in thought. Carmen occasionally hiccuped as her sobs died away.

Vincent realised that sometime in the last three days he had definitely fallen in love with Carmen. He didn't know exactly when, or why, but he had no doubt in his mind. She was deeply upset at the moment, but he knew he just wanted to protect and look after her, not just now, but always. His arms tightened around her and he kissed her forehead.

Carmen was deeply troubled. This had been her first job after graduating and it had all gone horribly wrong. Her chances of a good reference now were nil and any potential employer would want to know why she was changing jobs after only two months, so getting a new job was going to be tough. Without a paycheck, she would have to move back to her parent's house in North Hollywood. Everybody had been so proud of her graduating from Stanford and she thought they would see her now as a failure. To make matters worse, she had met this wonderful man and she wouldn't see him again. She looked up and him and said through trembling lips. "I'm not going to see you again am I?"

"Oh yes, you are!" said Vincent, giving her a squeeze, "now I've found you I'm not letting you go."

"But she fired me. We won't meet again. I have to find a new job and go back to live with my parents."

She slumped against Vincent and the tears started again.

Vincent stroked her hair and wiped her tears away.

"I have a much better plan," he said.

Carmen looked up at him with a red eyes and trembling lower lip.

Vincent cupped her chin in his hand and bent down to kiss her lightly on the lips.

"We both need a fresh start. Forget all this and put it behind you. I'm going to need a new publisher and so now I will become Valerie Kay with the full knowledge of whoever the new publisher turns out to be, and Carmen Castro can become my new agent."

Carmen hugged him. He was adorable.

"Oh Vincent, it's so sweet of you but you shouldn't feel sorry for me, I'll find a new job."

"Listen," he said, "I don't want to work with this publishing house anymore, because you're not going to be there and I really don't want to see or talk to Julia Wynne ever again. My contract is finished, so I'm free to walk away to another publisher. I want you to come with me and be my agent. Valerie is tired of pretending to be the author and has her own career to consider."

She looked up at Vincent while considering what he was saying. This was not at all what she had ever thought of doing.

"But I don't know anything about being a literary agent."

"You probably know more than you realise and I will help you. Valerie can teach you everything she's learnt in the last couple of years. We'll work together to find a new publisher for Valerie Kay. Then you can be available to represent other authors."

"But where would I do this?"

"In Wimbledon with me. If you want to come with me, of course."

"Come with you? You mean move to London and work for you?"

"Yes. Absolutely. Then we could start by looking for a new publisher in London or elsewhere in

England. Do you have a passport?"

"Yes, I have a passport, we went on vacation to Mexico two years ago."

Carmen fell silent while she thought through the ramifications of what he was suggesting. It was all a bit sudden.

Vincent didn't say anything while she thought about it, as he cuddled her to him.

"Would I live with you and Valerie? Suppose Valerie doesn't like me stealing her brother?"

"You can have the spare bedroom, there's plenty of room. Of course, I'm happy to share my room with you, but I realise you might want some space to call your own. And my sister? She will be eternally grateful if you take over and keep me organised. She only does it because I insisted. She's much more interested in her biochemistry lab and she'll probably enjoy having another girl around the house as well."

"Would I need a visa or something?"

"Not if you're just visiting. Why not come visit for a month or two? It will give you a chance to see if you like it there, see if we can find a new publisher and be sure we'll get along for more than just a long weekend. Once we're both sure it will work out, you can apply for a working visa. If it doesn't work out, you can just think of it as a vacation before you go home to find a new job."

Carmen snuggled into Vincent for a few minutes longer while she thought it over. The idea of spending more time with him was irresistible and giving her a warm feeling. She'd never met a man before who made her feel like this. The idea of going home with him was really good too, but then she suddenly sat up as something struck her.

"My mother will have a fit if I go to London with you," she said, looking back up at Vincent with a frown.

"So take me home to meet your mother and we'll explain it to her."

A small smile played on Carmen's face as she considered what he had said and then she laughed.

"It's crazy, but you *must* be serious about this if you want to meet my mother! Ok, lets do it. Can you come home with me tomorrow? You can meet my parents for a couple of days and if my mother doesn't chase you away with a kitchen knife, I'll pack my bags and go with you to London."

She pulled his head down for another kiss.

"In that case," said Vincent, as he came up for air a short while later, "I need to buy a new plane ticket, for the same flight as you, first thing in the morning. So we ought to get an early night."

"Yes, we should," said Carmen, sitting up to remove his tie and start working on his shirt buttons, "and if we have an early night, we might get enough sleep."

Chapter 14

Carmen and Vincent arrived at Los Angeles airport and decided to rent a car rather than take a cab. They needed to get to South Barrington Avenue and then to Carmen's office and back again. And tomorrow they planned to go North Hollywood to Carmen's parents' house. They left the rental car offices and walked with their bags to the parked cars.

"There it is," said Vincent, pointing, "it's the one right at the end."

Carmen looked at him quizzically.

"How do you know it's that one?" she asked.

"Because it's blue, the right model and the right registration plate on the front," replied Vincent, looking at Carmen.

He thought it was obviously the car and thus a rather odd question.

"You can see the numbers on the plate from here?" asked Carmen in a surprised voice.

"Yes, of course."

He stopped walking and turned to Carmen, "can't you?"

"Not very well, no," said Carmen squinting a little, "you have really good eyesight."

It was Vincent's turn to be surprised. They continued walking to the car and he wondered if Carmen's eyesight wasn't very good. It might explain some of the little accidents she had been having.

"Do you mind if I drive?" he asked as they reached the car, still thinking that her eyesight might not be very good.

"No, you go right ahead. I don't much care for driving, I always seem to end up a nervous wreck," said Carmen, putting her bag down at the car.

"But if you're going to drive, you had better go around to the left hand side of the car in this country."

Vincent smacked his forehead with the palm of his hand.

"Not a good start is it? Ok, Miss Carmen, in addition to navigating, you have to make sure I stay on the wrong side of the road."

"Wrong side? You mean the right side I hope!"

"Where I come from, the left hand side of the road is the right side and the right hand side of the road is the wrong side."

Vincent put their bags in the car and got behind the wheel.

"Vincent, am I safe with you driving? My mother told me never to get in a car with a strange man," said Carmen, as she slid into the passenger seat.

Vincent put his hand on her thigh and squeezed gently while staring into her eyes.

"My dear, after the last few days I don't count as a stranger any more, but it doesn't mean you're safe."

Carmen laughed and smacked his hand away.

"Just drive! Take a right out of the car park."

They left the car park and turned to the right onto the street.

"Are we going to your office first?"

"Yes, we are going to my *ex*-office first. I need to hand in my travel expenses, clear my desk and see if my pink slip is ready."

"What is your pink slip? It sounds like something you might wear."

"It's the piece of paper which says officially that I'm fired."

"It's all a bit sudden isn't it? Don't they have to give you notice or something?"

"Nope, I was on probation for three months and I've only been here two months, so they can throw me out instantly."

Carmen let out a long sigh.

"I'll come in with you for moral support," offered Vincent, reaching for her hand and holding it briefly.

Carmen thought about it for a few minutes as they made their way through the traffic heading north on the 405 freeway.

"I think you could do more than just offer moral support," said Carmen, looking across at him.

"Why don't I introduce you around as the author Valerie Kay? If you're really going to leave anyway, why don't we reveal your big secret and make Julia Wynne's day complete?"

Vincent grinned.

"It's a wicked idea, but I like it."

Carmen sat back in the car seat and repressed some small guilty feelings. Getting thrown out of the office after two months was a bit humiliating, but being escorted out on the arm of a blond hunk would definitely soften the blow. Some of her colleagues would be green with envy and probably think it was the real reason she was leaving. Carmen allowed herself a little smile and thought how if she was going, she wanted to go in style. She turned to Vincent.

"Vincent, I wonder if you could do something else for me?"

Vincent glanced at her.

"Of course, what is it?"

"When we're in the office, could you be sure to look at me in adoring sort of way? I want to make my colleagues jealous on my last day."

Vincent's eyebrows rose as they stopped at a red light. He put the car in park and turned to face Carmen.

"My dear, you are remarkably honest and totally evil, but I will have no difficulty in obeying your wishes. Nobody will doubt that I really am totally smitten with you."

He leant over and kissed her forehead just before the lights went green.

Chapter 15

When they got to her office, Carmen stopped by the photocopier to get an empty box. Then Carmen and Vincent went to her desk where she put all her personal items in the box.

"Hey, CC, what's happening?" said her friend Gloria, emerging from the adjacent cubicle.

"I got fired by Julia," replied Carmen, shrugging her shoulders ruefully.

"Oh no, that's too bad," said Gloria, putting her arms around Carmen and hugging her. As she did, and her mouth was close to Carmen's ear, she added, "we all know she's a bitch but there's nothing much we can do."

Gloria stepped back a little and looked at Carmen.

"Let us know where you go. If it's nice the rest of us might join you."

Then she then looked up at Vincent and smiled at him, before turning back to Carmen.

"Are you going to introduce me?"

"Of course," said Carmen. "Vincent, this is my good friend Gloria. Gloria this is Vincent Kingsley, also known around here as Valerie Kay."

"What? No way! Valerie Kay is a girl, I've spoken to her on the phone," said a sceptical voice from the small crowd which was gathering around them.

Vincent turned to face the person who had spoken.

"Well, yes, it's almost right, Valerie Kingsley certainly is a girl, she's my twin sister and up to now she's been the public face of Valerie Kay. And in public I've been introduced as Valerie Kay's agent. But the truth of the matter is, the author Valerie Kay is really me, Vincent Kingsley."

He gave them all a small bow from the waist.

"And now I would like to introduce you to my adorable new agent, Carmen Castro," he said with a theatrical flourish of both hands towards Carmen.

The noise level suddenly went up an order of magnitude as everybody exclaimed in surprise to each other at the news.

"Carmen, you mean you've quit?" said somebody from the back.

"Quit, no. Julia fired me, I've just come in to collect my stuff," answered Carmen honestly.

"Oh, no," said somebody else, "it's too bad, we'll miss you, why did she fire you?"

"Well," started Carmen with a sigh, "I had some little incidents and then finally I accidentally spilled a bottle of dark red wine over her brand new cream coloured outfit at the awards dinner."

"Damn," said another voice from the crowd into the hush, as people thought about it, "I wish I could have seen that."

There were quite a few sniggers, snorts and people trying not to laugh.

Vincent could see Julia was a very unpopular boss and any lingering doubts he had about going to a new publisher fled.

Something occurred to Gloria.

"Carmen, if you're going to be Vincent's agent and Vincent lives in London, England," she glanced at Vincent for confirmation, who nodded she was correct, "does it mean you're going to London too?"

"Yes, it's right," replied Carmen, putting her arm around Vincent's waist.

She looked up at him as he put his arm around her shoulders and smiled down at her. There was a collective sigh from the small crowd around them.

"Can I come too?" said someone and the others laughed.

Vincent looked over the group of girls and ladies looking at him and started to get the feeling of being hunted again. He moved behind Carmen, put his arms around her waist and pulled her back into him. Carmen put her hands over his, leant back and smiled up at Vincent who was gazing adoringly into her eyes. He pulled his eyes away, being obviously reluctant and looked back at the group while keeping hold of Carmen. He had their full attention now and more than one was staring at them with an open mouth and round eyes.

"Ladies," he said, and they quietened down.

"It has been a great pleasure meeting you, but we have much to do today. For a start, we have some paperwork to attend to upstairs, so we must bid you farewell. Perhaps we'll meet again at a convention or somewhere."

He blew a kiss to them all and they started to disperse back to their desks just as a phone rang somewhere. A few of her colleagues hugged Carmen as Vincent turned around and picked up the box of things from Carmen's desk.

A few minutes later they were upstairs at Patty's desk.

Chapter 16

As they approached Patty's desk, she looked up at Carmen, and then her eyes flicked with interest to Vincent. She glanced behind her, seeing the door to Julia Wynne's office was closed, before looking back to Carmen.

"I hear things didn't go quite according to plan in New York," she said, with obvious regret and a sad face.

"Well, no," replied Carmen ruefully, "it could definitely have been better."

She passed over the envelope of receipts and remaining cash to Patty. Patty emptied the envelope onto her desk, looked it briefly and pushed it all to one side. In return, she gave Carmen another envelope. Carmen looked inside, saw her termination paperwork with her final pay check and stuffed it into her purse.

"However, from what I hear, it wasn't all bad," said Patty, trying hard but not quite succeeding, in suppressing a smile as Carmen looked up again.

Carmen hesitated, as if she was not quite sure what Patty was meaning. Carmen looked sideways at Vincent, before looking back to Patty.

Patty didn't wait for a reply and looked at Vincent with interest.

"Are you going to introduce us?"

"Oh, excuse me," said Carmen. "Vincent, this is Patty, Julia Wynne's secretary. Patty this is Vincent Kingsley, also known as Valerie Kay."

Patty leant back in her chair, twirling a pencil in her fingers and regarding Vincent carefully. She narrowed her eyes at him.

"But Valerie Kay is a woman. I've spoken to her on the phone."

"Which is exactly what they said downstairs," said Vincent, with a grin.

"You spoke to my twin sister, Valerie Kingsley. Julia would never have signed a male author would she? However, in reality, I am the author known as Valerie Kay. Valerie, my sister, was only masquerading as Valerie Kay and at the same time I have been masquerading as Valerie Kay's agent. That's all over now, and Carmen here is Valerie Kay's new agent."

Patty's mouth dropped open and then a smile crept across her face.

"Does Julia know this?" she whispered.

There was the sound of an office door opening behind Patty and she sat up straight and blanked her face.

"No, but she's just about to find out," replied Vincent, as they all turned to face Julia.

Julia looked daggers at Carmen.

"Patty, if you've finished with Miss Castro, she can leave now."

She then turned to face Vincent, her face hardly softening.

"Give Mr Kingsley a copy of the new draft contract and we can sign it right now if he's agreeable."

She turned to go back into her office.

Vincent took hold of Carmen's hand.

"It won't be necessary. Miss Castro, my new agent, will be discussing my new contract with a different publisher."

Julia stopped and turned back, clearly puzzled and not understanding what he had just said.

"Goodbye Patty, it's been a pleasure meeting you," said Vincent, reaching forward to shake Patty's hand.

"Goodbye Vincent," said Patty, standing to shake his hand.

"I'm so pleased to have finally met Valerie Kay in person. You take good care of Carmen now."

She shook Carmen's hand and then Vincent and Carmen turned to walk down the hall to the lift.

Julia was standing there staring in amazement as they walked away. She finally turned to Patty.

"What did he mean? Was that really Valerie Kay? And he turned down a new contract without even reading it?"

"He means they're both leaving. And yes and yes," said Patty, answering all the questions while trying not to sound smug and pleased as well.

It wouldn't do to antagonise Julia, but it felt like a victory. A small victory perhaps, but a victory all the same. It was time somebody stood up to Julia.

Julia was still staring down the hall, struggling to understand and accept what had just happened. Finally she uttered a curse which Patty had never heard Julia use before, then went back into her office, slamming the door behind herself.

Chapter 17

Carmen and Vincent had arrived at South Barrington Avenue. Over pasta and a bottle of red wine, Carmen had explained her new circumstances to her two house mates. Since Carmen's rent was already paid for another month, they didn't have a problem with her leaving.

"Vincent, I'm going to call my parents now and tell them we're going to see them for a couple of days," said Carmen, picking up her phone.

"You are sure they'll be ok with that?" asked Vincent, as she dialled the number.

"Ok? My mother will probably be ecstatic when she hears I'm taking a man to meet her," said Carmen, turning away slightly as the phone was answered.

"Mamá, it's Carmen."

"Carmina! How was New York?"

"New York was ... interesting. I'll tell you all about it tomorrow when I see you."

"Oh wonderful, they gave you a couple of days off, I'll cook your favourites and you can tell me everything."

"Mamá, I'm bringing someone with me whom I'd like you to meet."

There was a slight pause in the conversation.

"Someone you want us to meet?" said Carmen's mother slowly, as she digested the information. "I think we shall be very pleased to meet him. Is he clever and good looking then?"

"Well, yes, but how did you know it was a man?"

"Carmina, why would you want us to meet this person if it was just a girl from the office? Is this someone you met in New York who lives here in California?"

"Yes, Mamá, we met in New York, but he's English and he's going back to London on Thursday. He wanted to meet you before he flies back home."

Carmen didn't want to tell her mother just yet that she was planning to go to England with him. She wasn't too sure of the reaction she would get from her parents, so it was definitely something to break to them face-to-face.

There was another slight pause in the conversation.

"In this case your father will take a two day vacation to meet him. What's his name?"

"Vincent Kingsley."

"Ok, you go and pack. I have to tell your father about his vacation and then we have to go to the supermarket to buy some food. You can tell Vincent I'll make sancocho for him. Besos, mi niña."

"See you tomorrow, besos, mamá."

Carmen put the phone down and turned to face Vincent.

"You are honoured. She's making sancocho for you, and she only does that on special occasions."

"What is sancocho?"

"It's a kind of beef stew with sweet potato, corn, onion, sweet peppers, potato, squash and all sorts of things. My mother makes it really well, you could say it's her speciality. She got the recipe from my grandmother who brought it with her from Puerto

Rico. All my grandparents came from Puerto Rico to California back in the 1920's so we have a lot of Puerto Rican food."

"It's sounds really nice, I'll look forward to it. Now I think it's my turn to phone home, otherwise Valerie is going to wonder why I didn't arrive."

"Good. You do that and I'll start packing. It's mostly clothes, books and music, so we can put it all in the car tomorrow."

*　*　*

Back in North Hollywood, Carmen's mother interrupted Carmen's father, who had been watching tv.

"Eduardo, Eduardo, Carmen is bringing a boy home to meet us," she said excitedly.

"Ah, Susana, finally!" said her husband. "I was beginning to despair of our daughter. The last time she brought a boy home she was still in High School, so she must be serious about this one," he said, with clear satisfaction in his voice.

"Oh yes, I think so. She said *he* wanted to meet *us*. So you need to take two days vacation but right now you go and put your shoes on. We have to go down to the supermarket to buy food."

Eduardo sighed. There was no way he was going to be able to see the rest of the tv program but it was in a good cause. He pushed himself out of the armchair and went in search of his shoes and credit cards.

Chapter 18

Vincent and Carmen were heading further up the 405 freeway with the back of the car full of bags and boxes. As Vincent drove, Carmen was thinking ahead to when her parents would meet him.

"Vincent, when my parents ask how we met, as I'm sure they will, I think we should just say how we met at breakfast on the first day."

"You don't think we should mention sharing a bedroom?" said Vincent, with a sly grin at her, "and how when we met we were wearing just one pair of pyjamas and a towel between the two of us?"

Carmen couldn't help snorting with laughter.

"My parents would have a fit. My mother would totally freak out and my father would go looking for his baseball bat."

"I'll take that as a 'no' then," said Vincent.

"But you will have to tell them about the incidents and how you got fired, won't you?"

Carmen sighed. Her parents had had great hopes for her after she had graduated from a university as prestigious as Stanford. Now she was going to disappoint them and feel like such a failure.

"Yes, it can't be avoided, but I'll tell my mother and then she can break it gently to my father, it will be better that way."

Vincent looked across the car at her.

"You told your mother you were bringing me to meet them, but did you say anything about going to London?"

Carmen hoped her parents wouldn't think she had gone completely off the rails.

"No, I thought it was enough shock that I was taking you to meet them."

"Shock? Why was it a shock? Because I'm English?"

"Because I never took a man home to meet them before."

She thought briefly about the boy in High School, but they had been teenagers and it was so long ago, he really didn't count.

"Not only that, but yes, you're English, living in London and you're a writer. Plus we've only known each other for five days and they are still thinking I am working for a publisher in LA."

Vincent drove quietly for a few minutes. Carmen glanced at him. He appeared to be thinking it over.

"They don't like writers?" he asked.

Carmen wasn't sure what he would think of Vincent being a writer. It wasn't the sort of issue which had arisen before, but her father could sometimes be very conventional and a bit old-fashioned in his ideas.

"My dad runs a construction company and my two brothers work for him. I'm not sure how he'll feel about a man driving a computer instead of a dump truck. You already know how people look down their nose at romance novels and he might have a problem with a guy writing them. I love him dearly, but he does have some fixed ideas about what is work for a man and work for a woman."

"In that case, we just tell him I write books. And if he asks, we tell him it's fiction. And then, if he asks what kind of fiction we try to change the subject."

Vincent looked across at Carmen, but she didn't

feel very convinced.

He continued, "maybe we should point out how my first three books are considered best sellers and if they keep on selling, I keep earning. He'll probably just assume I'm making a lot of money, even though I'm not."

"Lets hope he doesn't remember I was working for the Romance division and start to wonder how it all fits. At least you are established now, with books which sell, so you should be able to get a good advance with a new contract," said Carmen, as she thought it through.

"My brothers live nearby, so maybe my parents won't freak out if they think I'm moving to London. Hopefully they won't feel abandoned by all their children. We also have to tell them it's just temporary until we see how things go. Don't be surprised if they ask you if you've ever thought about moving to California."

They lapsed into silence, both wondering what reaction they would get.

Carmen was feeling nervous. There was her parents' reaction to deal with, then she was planning to go to a country she had never been to before, with no job, not much money and with a man she hardly knew. She was starting to wonder if this was a really stupid thing to do. It wasn't too late to back out and simply stay with her parents. She looked at Vincent and her heart ached. She had less than two days to decide if she should go with her head or her heart.

It was late morning when they arrived at Carmen's parents' house. As they pulled into the drive, Carmen's parents came out to greet them. Carmen's mother pulled Carmen into a hug and looked at Vincent over Carmen's shoulder.

"He's a good looking boy isn't he?" she said quietly into Carmen's ear, "he's tall and blond enough to be a Viking except he doesn't have a helmet with horns."

Carmen laughed and pulled back from her mother, turning to look over at Vincent and her father.

As Vincent stepped from the car, Carmen's father pulled him a hug and pounded him on the back.

"Vincent, welcome, welcome to our house," he said.

Vincent was caught by surprise, as he was not expecting a bear hug and to be thumped on his back. Not only that, but Eduardo had a heavy stubble on his chin. Even if he had shaved earlier that morning, by eleven o'clock the bristles were already showing again. Vincent felt as though somebody was rubbing a stiff scrubbing brush across his cheek. The look of shock on his face was enough to send Carmen and her mother doubled up into fits of laughter.

Eduardo turned to ask, "what? What?" while Vincent just stood there dazed.

Carmen and her mother recovered enough to wipe their eyes.

"Never mind, Eduardo, I'll tell you later," said her mother.

"Carmen, come and help me get lunch and you can tell me everything while we do it. The men can get your stuff from the car."

The women made their way into the house and Eduardo shrugged as if to say he didn't understand them. He turned to help Vincent get the bags from the car and stopped.

"Madre mia! What is all this? Why is there so much for two days?"

"Well...," said Vincent hesitantly, wondering how much to say at this point.

"She's moved out of her apartment, I'm sure she'll tell you all about it later."

To his relief, Eduardo just tsked with annoyance and started to unload the car.

96

Chapter 19

Lunch was at an end and they were finishing their coffee.

"Mrs Castro," said Vincent, "that was delicious, the best sancocho I have ever tasted."

Susana beamed, then pursed her lips and narrowed her eyes at Vincent.

"So when was the last time you had sancocho?"

"I cannot lie," said Vincent, shrugging and affecting innocence, "this is the first time, but it *was* truly delicious."

"Bah!" said Susana, batting him on the arm but smiling, "Eduardo, take this boy to the games room and play pool or something, Carmen and I have things to do in the kitchen."

"Do you play pool?" asked Eduardo, standing up.

"No, not these days, but I used to play snooker and some pool at college. I think I can remember how to play, it's not too difficult."

Vincent knew he was a better than average player of snooker, billiards and pool as well, but he wasn't going to say anything until he knew what he was up against.

"You watch out!" said Carmen to Vincent.

She pointed at her father.

"He's an expert, he nearly always beat us children at pool."

Carmen knew her father had some fixed ideas. He expected men to be interested in sport, drink beer and to know how to play games like baseball and pool. She was a bit worried. If Vincent was no good at pool, her father might view him with contempt, and it would be a bad start to the whole discussion of her going to London. She thought her father looked a bit smug as he guided Vincent to the games room.

Three hours later they came back to find the women sitting around the table.

Carmen thought her father didn't look smug any more.

"He beat me!" he said to them, "eight games to three! I think he is the expert, not me. You should have warned me," he said to Carmen, wagging a reproving finger at her.

"I had no idea," said Carmen, looking at Vincent in amazement, "he must be very good to beat you. I wonder what other talents he has which I don't know about yet."

"We have arroz con pollo and flan de leche for later," said her mother, changing the subject, "but first there are some things we need to talk about."

Vincent sat next to Carmen and she leaned over to whisper to him, "rice with chicken, then caramel custard, more traditional Puerto Rican dishes."

Vincent smiled in approval.

"Eduardo, I'll tell you and if I haven't got it right, Carmen will correct me."

Carmen nodded.

Eduardo also sat at the table and Susana told him how Carmen had met Vincent, lost her job and was going to London with him. Eduardo was taken aback more than once, but he waited until Susana had finished before asking any questions.

"How long are you going to London for?" he asked Carmen, immediately getting to the point which concerned him most.

"Just for a couple of months at first," said Carmen, taking Vincent's hand.

"In theory it's just a vacation and for a short while, so I don't need a work visa. In practice, I'll be helping Vincent, working out how to be his agent and seeing how everything else works out."

Vincent and Carmen looked at each other and smiled.

She continued, "and it will be a chance to do a little tourism, see how I like London and to meet Vincent's sister and his mother."

Eduardo pursed his lips for a moment while he looked at the pair of them and thought about what he had just been told. The others waited for him to speak.

"As I understand it," he said slowly, turning to Vincent, "writers don't make much money, especially in the early years and London's an expensive city, so how do you manage?"

"The house I share with my sister Valerie, we inherited from our grandmother, so there's no mortgage and we share the rest of the expenses such as utilities. Then there's a bus from the end of the road, it's only ten minutes walk to a major rail and tram station and therefore we don't need a car. So the expenses are relatively low and we manage pretty well. My sister has a well paid job and can easily pay her share of the expenses. I have three books which are selling well and a fourth just finished. You are right that it takes a while to get going as an author, but as my expenses are low, I'm already doing better than break even."

Eduardo said, "Hmm," to himself and then turned to his wife.

"Susana, why don't you show Vincent the rest of the house, while I have a word with Carmen?"

"Of course. Vincent, let me show you your room," said Susana, "I've put you in Roberto's old room which is next door to Carmen."

She ushered Vincent out and when they had gone and closed the door behind them, Eduardo turned to Carmen.

"This is a pretty big step, are you sure about this?"

Carmen reached across the table and squeezed her father's hand.

"Papá, I am pretty nervous but I have to give it a chance, otherwise I will always regret not trying it. If it doesn't work out I'll be back in a few weeks to live with you and mamá while look for a job here."

Eduardo looked thoughtfully at Carmen. He wasn't very comfortable with the idea, but he knew she would have to spread her wings and fly away at some point, probably with a husband. He just hadn't expected it to be now and, as well, travelling to an entirely different continent. Somehow he had always imagined it would be somewhere not too far away, like Santa Monica where she had been sharing a house. But she was smart and needed to know she would be welcome to come back if it wasn't working. He stood, came around the table and hugged her.

"I understand, and it reminds me a bit of what your grandparents did over eighty years ago."

He kissed her on her forehead and continued, "I'll put some money on your credit card before you go, so if you need to grab a bag and run to the airport to come home, you can. If you do, we will be happy to have you back and there will be no criticism. Sometimes you just have to take a chance, otherwise like you say, you will always regret and wonder what might have happened. If you want to go, you can go with my blessing. If you change your mind before you get on the plane, that's ok too."

"I don't think I'll suddenly need to run to the airport to come home, but thank you anyway," Carmen reached up and kissed her father's cheek.

"If you don't, then you have some money to keep you going until you start earning money," said Eduardo said gruffly, finding his throat a little tight.

"Let's go find this boy of yours and see if they got to the swimming pool yet."

Chapter 20

Vincent and Carmen arrived in Murray Road, Wimbledon, by cab from the station. It wasn't far, but they had had a long and mostly sleepless overnight journey from California. Consequently they were much too tired to consider walking there, especially pulling two suitcases, even if the cases did have wheels. In Murray Road, Vincent paid the cab as Carmen looked around wide-eyed. She'd seen England and London in the movies, but it wasn't the same as actually being here. She thought it looked quite different from North Hollywood or Santa Monica.

The cab drove off and she followed Vincent as he walked up the garden path of a substantial Victorian semi-detached house. As he reached to put his key in the lock, the door was opened by a blond girl who looked remarkably like Vincent. Carmen realised immediately this had to be Valerie and there had been no reason for a momentary flicker of jealousy. The twins hugged and as Valerie looked over his shoulder, she blinked to see Carmen standing behind him holding her suitcase.

"Vincent," cried Valerie, standing back a little, "you told me about Carmen, but you never said you were bringing her home! You bad boy!"

She pushed past him to Carmen.

"Hello, I'm Valerie, Vincent's twin, and you must be Carmen. I'm so pleased to meet you!"

She kissed Carmen on the cheek.

Carmen was greatly relieved to be welcomed immediately. Vincent had said it would be fine, but there had been a little niggling worry at the back of her mind about intervening between twins.

"I'm pleased to meet you," she said to Valerie, "I hope you don't mind me coming with Vincent?"

"Mind? Goodness me no," said Valerie, "I'm glad to see you, I just hope you can keep him away from the computer from time to time. He needs to get out more, so perhaps he will now you are here. Anyway, enough talking at the door. Let me take your case and you go ahead into the house."

Carmen followed Vincent, who was already in the hallway and embracing an older lady, presumably his mother.

Vincent had gone inside and kissed his mother on the cheek. He had hoped to make the necessary explanations to his mother once he was over the worst of his jetlag. Finding her waiting here when he got home hadn't been in the plan.

"Mum, I've brought someone home with me from America whom I want you to meet. I was going to take her over to meet you tomorrow, once we'd had a shower and a nap."

They turned to face Carmen as she came down the hallway, while Valerie closed the front door behind them.

"Mum, I'd like you to meet Carmen Castro. Carmen, this is my mother and I think Valerie already introduced herself. Mum, Carmen is going to be staying with us for a while. She will be helping me find a new publisher for my books and acting as my agent from now on."

His mother's eyebrows rose slightly, as clearly

she didn't think it was the whole story.

"Well, that's nice dear, now you won't have to keep pestering Valerie to help you."

"And thank goodness for that," added Valerie, "I shall be happy to pass it all on to you Carmen!"

"Now then," said Vincent's mother, "I'll put the kettle on for a cup of tea, while you two go upstairs and freshen up. Then you can both come down and tell me all about it."

Vincent shrugged and pulled a face at Carmen which said, 'this is all out of my control for the moment, lets just do what she says.'

He reached for Carmen's suitcase.

"Come on, I'll show you to your room, then we can take quick showers before we come down again."

Philippa Carey

Chapter 21

The next morning, Carmen went down to the kitchen to find Vincent making coffee. She glanced at the clock on the wall as she sat down at the kitchen table.

"Ten o'clock already! I suppose Valerie has gone to work?" she said.

"Yes, she's back at work, now she's more or less over the flu. She's probably feeling washed out, as you do after flu, but she's very keen on their latest project."

"I did think I heard someone moving about before, but I just went back to sleep."

"We'll have to make an effort to get up earlier tomorrow, otherwise it will take ages to get over the jetlag. It always seems worst going from west to east."

"What's the plan for today?"

"Not a lot, but we should probably get you signed up with the RNA."

"RNA?"

"Romantic Novelists Association. It's like the Romance Writers of America, but a bit more restrictive. To join the RNA you have to have been published, or be in their limited New Writer Scheme or else be employed in the industry. In your case you will be eligible as my agent."

"Why do I need to join?"

"Because you'll be able to attend their meetings and get to know lots of people. It's a very supportive organisation run by authors for authors."

"Will you be around to introduce me?"

"I will, but there's no need. They're such a friendly bunch they'll introduce themselves, as you'll find out. In the meantime, lets get dressed and I'll take you for a walk on the common."

Vincent turned and peered out of the kitchen window.

"It's a bit cloudy, but not raining."

Carmen wondered if you always had to check the weather in this country. She had heard it rained a lot. So why hadn't she brought a rain coat with her? Where were the shops in Wimbledon? Was there a clothing store?

"Vincent, I didn't bring a raincoat with me. Is there a shopping mall here?"

"Yes, there is, right by the station. We can walk there. At the same time, we should go to the library in the town centre as well, to see if they have a copy of The Writers and Artists Yearbook. You'll need to make a list of publishers, although Valerie might already have done so."

Carmen relished the prospect of starting afresh with a new job. She might miss Gloria's company, but being with Vincent and Valerie felt like a good exchange. She yawned. She needed to clear the cobwebs from her head.

"I'm going to shower and get dressed," she said, "then let's go for that walk, I need some fresh air to wake me up properly."

"We could stop at a pub on the common for an early lunch," said Vincent, "I don't feel like cooking today."

"Will I have to get used to warm beer now?" asked Carmen.

"Not really warm, but cool rather than ice cold. If it's too cold, your taste buds freeze, so you can't taste it and you will definitely want to taste our beer."

As Carmen went upstairs to the shower, she reflected how life here was going to be very different from California. She hoped she would grow to like it.

Chapter 22

A month later, on a sunny Friday afternoon, Vincent and Carmen were sitting on a bench at the bottom of the garden. Recent showers had finally given way to sunshine. They were taking a break and drinking tea in the shade of an old apple tree.

"How do you like Wimbledon, now you've been here a few weeks?" asked Vincent.

"It's nice, but I would like it a bit better if it was warm more of the time and rained a little less," replied Carmen, smiling, "but there are some nice shops. It's also convenient for doing the tourist things in the centre of London or walking on the common."

She was wondering, with a little flame of hope in her heart, if this conversation was leading somewhere. She certainly knew where she wanted it to lead, and it involved her staying in Wimbledon for much longer than a few weeks.

"If it were the case, the grass and the trees might not be so green, but as it is, could you imagine living here?"

"Oh yes," answered Carmen with truthful enthusiasm.

The little flame of hope grew a little larger and she decided to hint a little.

"It would depend on the circumstances of course, but yes."

She was starting to feel a little excitement about what might be coming next.

"In this case, Miss Castro," said Vincent, more than a little nervously, "I have to tell you I love you very much. I would be deeply honoured and very happy if you would marry me."

Carmen squealed, jumped up, plonked herself down in his lap, threw her arms around his neck and kissed him enthusiastically. A few minutes later they came up for air.

"Can I take that as a yes?" asked Vincent.

"Yes, yes, yes," said Carmen before kissing him long and hard again.

When they came up for air a second time, Vincent said, "In this case I have a little something for you in my pocket, if you would just stand up for just a moment."

Carmen promptly stood up and looked down eagerly, as Vincent reached into his pocket. He withdraw a small jewellers box which he flipped open to show Carmen a ring. It was a diamond with two smaller sapphires each side of it. He took it from the box and as Carmen held out her left hand, which was trembling a little, he put the ring on her finger.

"It's beautiful," she breathed, studying it carefully.

"It's four o'clock now, so it's eight in the morning in California. Shall we call your parents?"

In reply, Carmen grabbed his hand and ran back into the house with him to find the phone.

The End

But keep on reading for a Sancocho recipe...

Puerto Rican Sancocho

Sancocho is a very varied dish, popular across Latin America and the Canary Islands. From every person you ask, you will get a different version. This is one of the simpler versions to give you an idea. I apologise to my non-American readers as this recipe uses cups, spoons and pounds as I could not find a recipe which also used grams and millilitres. I considered attempting a conversion of the units, but thought it would probably then be a recipe for disaster....

Ingredients

2 tablespoons Olive Oil
5 cloves Garlic, minced
1½ pounds Top Round (Rump) Beef, cut into 1 inch cubes
⅓ cups Onions, diced
⅓ cups Green Peppers, diced
5 sprigs Cilantro (Coriander leaf), chopped
1 teaspoon Salt
¼ teaspoons Ground Pepper
4 whole Tomatoes, medium, cored and chopped
4 quarts Beef Stock, divided
1 whole Green Plantain, peeled and cut
1 whole Yellow Plantain, peeled and cut
1 whole Sweet Potato, medium, peeled and diced
½ pound Butternut Squash, peeled and cubed into 1 inch pieces
3 whole Potatoes, medium, peeled and

quartered
    2 ears Yellow Corn, cleaned, and cut into 6 parts

Method

In a heavy (casserole) pot over low-to-medium heat, combine olive oil, garlic, beef cubes, and onions. Stir until beef is brown on all sides and onions begin to caramelize. Add in chopped pepper, cilantro, salt, ground pepper, tomatoes, and 1 quart of beef stock. Cook down until stock is reduced by half, about 20 minutes.

Stir beef, then add in all the remaining ingredients and beef stock. Continue to cook until meat is tender and the vegetables are soft.

About the Author

Philippa Carey also graduated from Cambridge University, like Valerie and Vincent, but as a Software Engineer and not from Clare College. Philippa is now semi-retired, writing and living near Cambridge in the United Kingdom.

Philippa is a member of the Romantic Novelist's Association and RNA author profiles can be found here:
www.romanticnovelistsassociation.org/rna_author

Sadly, neither Vincent Kingsley nor Valerie Kay can be found via the link. This is, after all, a work of fiction.

Look for more of Philippa's novels and novellas, which are set in a mixture of The Regency, the Victorian era and the present day.

Philippa will be eternally grateful if you would leave a review of this story at your favourite book website.

More of Philippa's books can be found at
www.pcarey.uk

www.ingramcontent.com/pod-product-compliance
Lightning Source LLC
Chambersburg PA
CBHW031309060726
47590CB00003B/1126